# THE JOY RIDERS

SUSPENSE

# THE JOY RIDERS

## WILLIAM BEDFORD

mammoth

First published in Great Britain 1998
by Mammoth, an imprint of Reed International Books Limited
Michelin House, 81 Fulham Road, London SW3 6RB

ISBN 0 7497 3480 9

10 9 8 7 6 5 4 3 2 1

A CIP catalogue record for this title is available from the British Library

Typeset by Avon Dataset Ltd, Bidford on Avon, Warwickshire
Printed in Great Britain by Cox & Wyman Ltd, Reading, Berkshire

*For Jo*

*September 5th 1973 – October 30th 1988*

# One

I was furious all the way down to the Pier.

'After everything I've told you,' I shouted as we pedalled through the evening streets, dodging the traffic, weaving through the fumes of the queuing cars. 'After everything I've said about cigarettes. You must be totally stupid.'

Ben was upset and out of breath. He was on the verge of tears. I could tell from the way his mouth trembled and he kept staring fixedly ahead, refusing to look at me.

'All right, Jo, don't go on about it.'

'Somebody has to go on about it,' I yelled, working myself up even further.

'I promise . . .'

'You don't know the meaning of the word,' I reminded him unkindly. 'You *promised* last week. I can't believe anything you say.'

'It doesn't count when you threaten somebody,' Ben gasped, struggling to keep up. 'It isn't fair.'

I scoffed at that. He was talking about the morning when I took his new Gameboy down to the pawnbrokers and threatened to sell it if I ever found him near a cigarette. The pawnbroker was perfectly happy to play along. We'd got our mountain bikes from him the previous year when Mum had double shifts at the Cineplex and a month in the fish fingers factory. Half the things we owned came from or ended up on his shelves.

'I'll more than threaten you!' I said angrily.

I know I sounded ridiculous, like I was trying to sound grown-up. But I wasn't going to stop. You reach a point with anger where you can't stop, and don't really want to, like being on a terrifying helter-skelter.

I could feel the cigarettes in my pocket. I knew Ben was frightened, and it wasn't really his fault. Everybody in our school smokes, and the girls laugh at you if you don't. They would have made Ben's life a misery if he hadn't tried. But I couldn't relent. I couldn't pretend it hadn't happened. I could sense Ben's tearful indignation, and when we slowed down at the traffic lights I could see there were tears in his eyes. But I didn't want to look at them. I had to keep my anger burning.

'It would break Mum's heart if she found you smoking,' I said self-righteously. The words lashed at him, bullying and unfair.

'What do you care?' he managed to say through his choked-up tears. 'You smoke!'

'I care because you're eleven and I'm fourteen,' I said pompously, 'and as far as Mum is concerned that means I'm the responsible one. I'm my brother's keeper. There's nobody else around to do the job. So you'd better be terrified.'

I ignored the jibe about my own smoking habits. He didn't speak after that. He kept staring ahead and fighting back the tears.

We cycled on to the Pier and right out to the end. The gates are left open all year now. No point locking them when kids keep smashing them down with stolen cars. We cycled out to the deserted end and I leaned my bike against the pavilion. Ben leaned his bike next to mine and stood with his back to me, staring out to sea. There were lots of ships at the estuary, waiting for a pilot to take them up to the commercial docks. The estuary curved round to the west, so that the promenade met the deep waters of the sea at its far end. Ben pretended to be interested in the sea while I struck matches and lit one of the cigarettes.

'Here you are,' I said.

He turned and looked at me. The cigarette was one of his, from the packet I had found in the computer disk drawer. I don't know where he got the money from, but they were unfiltered, strong and full of tar.

'I don't want it,' he said.

'Yes you do.'

'I don't.'

'You bought them.'

'I didn't.'

'You mean you stole them!'

'No, Jo!' he pleaded. 'You know I didn't steal them.'

'A fairy gave them to you?'

'All the kids at school do it.'

'You don't have to be like them.'

'I don't want it, Jo.'

'Smoke!' I said in my best grown-up voice, the one I use for answering the telephone (when it isn't disconnected, that is).

Ben took the cigarette and studied it as if we were doing some sort of scientific experiment in chemistry. He managed to study the cigarette until it went out.

'I don't know what to do with it,' he said innocently.

He has an innocent smile, my brother Ben, the kind of smile bullies want to pulverise the minute they see it. He's a sweet kid. He has blond curly hair to go with the innocent smile, and pink cheeks even in this day and age. You wouldn't believe he could come from where we live, the tower blocks down by the docks. I almost stopped. But I didn't.

'You try it, Ben,' I said, leaning forward with a scowl and lighting the cigarette again.

He held the cigarette to his lips and blew. A shower of sparks flew into my face, singeing my eyebrows and burning my lips. Ben laughed as I leaped about, brushing the sparks off my T-shirt.

'Idiot.'

'I told you . . .'

'You don't know what to do, yeh yeh. Inhale, you idiot.'

He stared at the cigarette in amazement, as if he had never seen one before. He put it in his mouth and took a long deep drag. Then he swallowed. When he opened his eyes they were lakes of pain. He choked and gasped for air. Smoke poured out of his nose and mouth and he yelped and danced around, flinging the cigarette over the Pier railings to the sea. I watched the tiny burning pinpoint somersault in the air and float down to the brown water where a massive herring gull swallowed it and then shrieked in agony, dive-bombing the Pier and disappearing over the horizon.

I couldn't stop laughing. I thumped Ben on the back and danced around with him, both of us yelling like Apaches looking forward to a bit of warfare.

'I hate it,' Ben said when he could speak again.

'Good.'

'It hurts.'

'It does, yes.'

'I don't know why you do it.'

I don't know myself, but I'm not going to admit that to my brother. I smoke because everybody else does. Including our mum, who threatens to kill me if Ben follows her example. It's great being fourteen when your baby brother is eleven and your mother has to find somebody to blame. I smoke because everybody else does, but it's my job to prevent my brother going down the same smokers' gangplank.

'I will never smoke again,' Ben told me solemnly.

'I hope that's the truth.'

'I will die before I smoke another cigarette.'

'You needn't go that far.'

We smiled at each other. I could have given him a hug, but he wouldn't have liked it. I knew there was a stupid smile on my face, but I couldn't stop smiling. I love him really.

Then we heard the car.

# Two

The car hit the promenade like a bomb.

It was a red Metro.

THWACK.

The rear end slammed into a traffic island and the orange beacon on the bollard blinked like a Dalek having a nightmare: attack, attack.

Turning left, the Metro hit second gear and roared down the middle of the road. There was no traffic. No tourists. Two seagulls squabbling round the rubbish bins rose in panic, screeching at the loud monster, and wheeling noisily away towards the foreshore.

The Metro must have been doing forty in second gear before it crashed up into third gear and aimed for the horizon – which was a ten-foot drop into the sea at the end of the promenade. You could hear the gears protesting. Black smoke poured out of the exhaust.

The first retarder sent the Metro two feet in the air.

CRASH.

It landed with a sickening thump.

'Twockers,' I said under my breath.

Ben leaned out over the Pier railings, waving his arms and shouting encouragement. He had forgotten all about his burning throat and sore eyes. He was screaming with excitement. I put my hand on his shoulder but kept my eyes on the Metro. There was no point spoiling his fun.

The Metro took three retarders in fourth gear, eating eighty miles an hour of cold autumn seaside air. Swarms of seagulls circled above the promenade, alarmed by the explosion of noise. A woman on a bicycle fled for the sands, leaving her bicycle to defend itself. The Metro took a sharp swerve to the right to destroy the abandoned bicycle and then raced away to wreck another retarder.

The retarder wrecked the Metro.

You could hear the guts of the engine being wrenched about. The suspension twanged like an electric guitar. Gears squealed hot iron arias. You could smell rust and flame.

'Twockers,' I said again under my breath.

You could tell it was twockers: taking without the owner's consent. No owner would consent to this degree of torture. This was one red Metro that wasn't going to fetch its catalogue price at any sale in town. As far as I could see, this was a dead Metro.

But the twockers were having fun.

They reached the end of the promenade and turned round on two squealing wheels, then came to a halt. The promenade was two miles long, but we could still hear the gunning of the engine. A storm of angry seagulls flew low over the throbbing monster, decorating it with white gifts. The woman on the sands climbed up to the promenade and kneeled in stunned shock beside her demolished bicycle.

In my bones, I knew who was in the car. Who else would twock a red Metro and then race it along a promenade which ended in a ten-foot drop into the sea?

The brothers Grim.

My head felt strange. Terrified. We shouldn't have gone down to the Pier, my little brother and I. I should have known better.

In the distance, the engine gunned again. Hot iron on maniac mile.

And I was worried about cigarettes!

Wow.

Then we heard the clang of gears. They were coming.

There was no time to run, and nowhere to run *to* even if we found the time.

# Three

The red Metro ghosted back along the promenade, past the amusement arcades and candyfloss stalls, a sad memory of the family car it used to be. It clanked and steamed, and as it approached the slipway before the Pier, slowed down to a clattering juddering crawl, letting out a mechanical whine like a rusty ship's siren. When it reached the Pier, it stopped. For a moment, I thought the engine was dead, that the twockers had killed it. But after a brief silence, the engine hummed into life again and the Metro turned slowly through the Pier gates.

'I knew they were going to do that,' I said, not really talking to Ben, just thinking aloud.

Ben moved a little closer. We stood side by side, with nowhere to go except over the end of the Pier.

Slowly, the Metro drove towards us. When it reached the end of the Pier, it shuddered and came to a halt.

I could hear Marillion wailing on the car's radio, the volume turned so loud that the radio had developed a cough. The car door opened and the sound increased, startling dozens of seagulls off the Pier roof. The seagulls circled noisily away towards the tideline, but Ben and I didn't have that option. We were left behind, abandoned, face to face with the brothers Grim.

They got out of the car.

Ash and Rainbow. The most dangerous pair of hooligans in our town.

Rainbow was holding a six-pack, struggling to open one of them with his teeth. 'Argghhh,' was Rainbow's favourite sentence. He was a real technicolour nightmare, sixteen years old with the sides of his head shaved and a long Mohican stripe dyed orange and electric green and stiff with gel. He had tattoos on his tattoos. His nose looked as if it had been broken several times in the fights he always seemed to enjoy. He was very big, Rainbow, a ton of painted muscle and headbanging resentment.

But the worst thing of all about Rainbow was that he fancied me. He had fancied me for months. When he saw me on the estate, he waved hello. In town, he grinned at me and whistled. The last time I ever saw him at school, he offered me a can of lager he'd only half finished. I didn't know which was more frightening: having him threaten to beat me up or go speechless with lovey-dovey grins.

Rainbow was staring at my cropped hair, frayed jeans and DM boots. My old anorak was scruffy and colourless. I always cut my own hair. It isn't blond like Ben's or Mum's, it's auburn and tightly curled and untidy. I hate it. Cutting it myself goes with the frayed jeans and DMs. It makes me feel I can manage.

'Ent you heard, Jo?' Rainbow said, frowning as if he couldn't believe my appearance. 'Tough has gone rainbow these days. Tough has gone technicoloured.'

I forced a smile onto my face. At least Rainbow recognised I was trying to look streetwise. But my smile creaked with the effort. I actually wanted to cry.

Rainbow laughed explosively at his own joke.

'It's Jo,' he told his angelic brother, Ash, who

was climbing leisurely out of the Metro.

Ash leaned into the car and killed Marillion. He smiled at his colourful brother. 'I know Jo when I see Jo,' he said flatly. He had a hard, evil voice, Ash, no humour, nothing human in it at all. When he sang the hymns in assembly, the hall went quiet. His drone was like a dentist's drill. Even the teachers stopped singing.

Ash wasn't colourful. He's the only sixteen year-old I know with grey hair. I don't know if he dyes it. Nobody has ever had the nerve to ask. Ash's face was grey, humourless, lifeless: like his eyes. And he was wearing his usual grey clothes: designer jeans and sweatshirt, always in grey; black and grey trainers. It was the total lack of colour that was the most frightening thing about Ash. It suggested worlds of woe and graveyard misery you couldn't begin to imagine. But Ash could. He could invent graveyard misery at will.

'Hello, Jo,' Ash said, his voice cold and unfriendly.

'Hello, Ash.'

'Wot you doin'?'

'Nothing.'

That, apparently, was a very funny answer.

Rainbow nearly choked on his beer. A nerve at the side of Ash's face trembled amid the pale wastelands of his sharp-boned cheeks.

'Jo's teaching me how to smoke,' Ben said proudly.

We all glanced at Ben. I thought I was teaching him how not to smoke, but this wasn't the time for an argument.

'Did it speak?' Ash said in his flat unfriendly way.

'Yeh,' Rainbow said. 'It did.'

'I'm not an it,' Ben said indignantly.

I trembled inside. I had no idea how Ash would react to hearing his brother contradicted.

But Ash wasn't in too bad a mood. He shook his head and sighed. He smiled at Ben. 'Courageous,' he said to his brightly deranged brother.

'Heroic,' Rainbow nodded in agreement.

In the silence, Rainbow's beer can frothed all over his jeans. Rainbow looked startled, glaring at the can, and I thought he was going to hurl it at one of the seagulls, but instead he offered it to Ash.

Ash drank with theatrical slowness, enjoying the tension. I heard the beer going down his throat like water gurgling in a sink. Rainbow got another can open and copied his brother.

Out of the corner of my eye, I saw a police car drive down to the promenade, turn left, and travel slowly through the evening stillness. In my mind, I was having a strange fantasy in which Ben said something else ridiculous and the brothers Grim lost their tempers on the end of the Pier, throwing us to a violent death while the police car drove silently out of view.

I don't know whether Rainbow and Ash even saw the car. They concentrated on emptying their cans of beer, and then tossed the empties over the railings to the sea surging darkly far below.

'OK,' Rainbow said, nodding at his brother.

'OK,' Ash agreed.

The police car reached the end of the promenade, turned round and came back. It passed the Pier without so much as a glance in our direction. If we had been boy scouts singing hymns they would have come and stopped us for breach of the peace. Because we were teenagers, drinking, hanging about on the Pier, apparently in possession of a car, they left us alone. Rainbow and Ash still hadn't seen them, or were pretending they weren't there. The police car turned back up the hill to town and disappeared without so much as a friendly wave.

'I got a thought,' Rainbow suddenly said excitedly. He leaned back inside the car and brought out a bottle of Diamond White. He offered me the bottle. I drank. It made me feel sick but I didn't show it. I handed the bottle back. 'Twockin',' Rainbow said as he took the bottle.

'Twocking,' I nodded.

'You ever been twockin', Jo?'

'I can't drive.'

They both laughed in amazement at that, as if I were the only person they'd ever met who couldn't drive a car.

'She can't drive,' Rainbow roared.

'She can't drive,' Ash beamed.

'It's true,' Ben said. 'Anyway, it's illegal when you're fourteen. You can't drive until you're seventeen.'

I could murder Ben sometimes. He's right but he's wrong if you know what I mean.

But Rainbow wasn't interested in Ben. 'We could

*show* you all about twockin',' he said with huge delight.

I shrugged and smiled and prayed. I didn't want to do anything with them. I certainly didn't want to see how they stole cars. I wanted to go home for my tea.

Ash frowned. He suddenly became serious. 'We don't make this offer to many people,' he said.

'I know that, Ash,' I said with a smile. 'I appreciate you offering . . .'

'I ent offering.'

'Great, yes.' I decided to stop talking. Maybe they would go away, like hayfever.

'Tonight then?' Ash resumed.

'Yes,' I nodded.

'Jo!' Ben protested.

'Shut up.'

'Yeh, shut up, gawk.'

'I'm not a gawk.'

'Kill the gawk, Rainbow.'

Ben climbed up on to the railings. 'I'll jump,' he threatened.

The brothers Grim loved that. 'Jump!' they yelled simultaneously. 'Jump!'

I stepped forward. 'Tonight?' I said quickly.

Ash turned his doleful stare back in my direction. 'That's right, Jo.'

'Where?'

'Tesco car park.'

'Jo!' Ben went on protesting.

I bent Ben's fingers back so far it hurt even me. He shrieked, then went quiet. That made Rainbow laugh. Ash looked interested, a flicker of life in his lifeless eyes.

'What time?' I asked.

'Just be there, Jo. You can guess the time. Part of the game, the uncertainty. Keep you on your toes. Long as it's before midnight. We turn into vampires at midnight. We turn into something nasty.'

'OK.'

'Get it wrong, we manure you.'

*Manure* me? I hope I never do anything sufficiently wrong to find out what that means.

Ash got back into the Metro and Rainbow followed him, bumping his head on the door. He thumped the roof and a shape like a fist appeared in what was left of the metallic surface.

'OK,' Ash yelled.

'OK,' Rainbow roared.

They reversed off the Pier in a cloud of fumes and smoke.

Ben and I were alone.

# Four

I couldn't wait to get home. We cycled as fast as we could along the promenade and then across the sands to the old fish docks. The fish docks are redundant now. They are planning to use them for a marina. We live in one of the tower blocks behind the old quays and fish market. Ben was gasping for breath by the time we crossed the sands, wanting to rest. I just wanted to be safe at home behind securely locked doors.

When we got to the tower block, the lifts were out of order. We had to carry the bikes all the way up to our flat on the eighth floor. Our mum can't stand heights, but the council refuse to move us because vertigo isn't a medical priority.

I was fighting for breath by the time we reached our corridor.

I knew Mum would be in a bad mood. She is always in a bad mood on Thursdays. She gets her wages in the afternoon, and it's never enough to live on, even when she works overtime. Then the manager starts making jokes, asking her which bloke she's living with these days. I don't think she's looked at a bloke since the day Dad walked out. The manager ruins her week, every week, with his snide remarks. And on top of that, we were late for supper. We couldn't afford to burn fish fingers in our house. Six burnt fish fingers and we were in trouble for the rest of the week.

But it wasn't fish fingers Mum had on her mind.

'I can smell the tobacco on your clothes,' she shouted the minute we walked through the door. 'I can smell it from here.'

I was stunned. Her own clothes reek like a cigarette factory working overtime, and yet she can detect a whiff of smoke on *Ben's* clothes!

'Leave it out, Mum, please,' I pleaded, but she was furious.

'No, I will not *leave it out*,' she said, grabbing hold of Ben and smothering him as if he'd just come back from the casualty ward at the hospital. 'I don't go to work for you to waste your brother's life smoking cigarettes,' she yelled. 'I told you . . .'

She didn't finish the sentence. She was crying, her shoulders shaking with emotion and exhaustion. She looked really tired. Her face was white with the strain of living with us. I knew I was to blame. I was always to blame. She held Ben in her arms and rocked him against her chest, mascara-blackened tears running down her face. She wears lots of mascara to hide her tiredness.

Our mum's name is Diane. She works as an usherette in the Cineplex and smokes twenty cigarettes a night because she can't stand the sort of films they show: murder and mayhem and weepy love stories. She wears seconds from the street market and factory reject shoes. Her best coat is the parka my dad left behind when he signed on to an oil tanker headed for Peru and never came back. I was seven when he left. I think about him every night. I'm sure the coat still smells of Dad when it rains.

'I won't do it again, Mum,' Ben said, struggling

24

to free himself from her passionate embrace.

'I know, sweetheart.'

'It was horrible. It made me cough.'

I stood at the window looking down to the docks. We live on the east side of the tower block and from our sitting room you can see the chemical works along the riverbank and the sprawling commercial docks, and far away at the estuary, the lighthouse. On foggy nights you can hear the foghorns on the river and out at the estuary. Smoke from the stubble-burning across the river darkens the sky every September. I grew up with this dramatic, panoramic view. I thought it was the most wonderful place in the world, until Dad went to Peru.

'It's a daft thing to do, Mum,' Ben was explaining. 'I know it kills you. Only stupid people smoke.'

'That's right, sweetheart,' Mum agreed, lighting up absent-mindedly and going to put the kettle on. The fish fingers were under the grill, waiting to be cooked. At least we hadn't ruined a day's food.

I stayed at the window. A car ferry was entering the main lockpit. I could hear the sirens, see the men waiting on the quays. Hundreds of cars are unloaded every week, and timber, steel, chemicals, oil from all over the world. We even get coal from Australia now all our own mines are closed. Sometimes, I wonder whether my dad is on one of the vessels lining up to be unloaded, but I know that isn't likely. People don't come back after seven years. Once they've left, they disappear.

I took the mug of tea and avoided my mum's eyes. She stood at my side, smoking her cigarette. Her temper had evaporated as rapidly as her wages. Ben was watching a video.

'You shouldn't smoke in the flat,' I said. 'You can't expect Ben not to smoke when you do it all the time.'

She sighed unhappily. 'I know, Jo. I'm sorry, I just can't . . .' She didn't finish the sentence, but I knew she couldn't manage without cigarettes, like some people can't manage without drink. She hates herself for it.

'I was trying to stop Ben,' I said. 'Show him how stupid it is.'

'I know, love.'

Ben shouted across the room without taking his eyes off *Jurassic Park.* 'Rainbow and Ash were on the Pier,' he said.

Mum glanced at me nervously. She didn't like Rainbow and Ash. 'Is that right, sweetheart?'

'They were funny.'

'The moronic orphans,' I said sourly under my breath.

Everyone knew about Ash and Rainbow. They were born on one of the big estates on the edge of town. Their mother worked on the fish docks, and ended up running away with a fish merchant who had an expensive car. She moved up to Aberdeen and never wrote, never even sent a Christmas card. She hadn't wanted children, she told Ash and Rainbow. They stayed with their father. He was a filleter on the fish market until the drink made him incapable of holding a sharp knife without cutting himself. He was sacked, and spent all his time drinking. He sang sentimental songs when he was drunk, and then went round the house wrecking the furniture.

When Ash and Rainbow were in primary school their father locked himself in the garage and put a garden hose in the car exhaust. He made sure there was plenty of petrol. Coming home from school, Ash and Rainbow found him dead in the car, a bottle of whisky gripped tightly in his left hand, a photograph

27

of *them* on the dashboard. After that, Ash and Rainbow went into care for a few weeks until their grandma could look after them. She was on holiday in Benidorm when their father died, and refused to come back for the funeral. When she eventually came home they left the estate and moved to the tenements near the docks.

Which was where I met them. We went to the same school. I knew all the horrible details of Ash and Rainbow's traumatic childhood in a heart-broken home. I heard their story every day in the playground, or read it in the local newspaper. I saw most of it. They grew up in hell, living with their grandma and then in a series of homes after she died. That was two or three years ago. I had no idea where they lived now, in foster care somewhere on one of the estates where nobody cared about anything. They had a terrible childhood. But it didn't mean I had to like them. Most of the kids in our school were having terrible childhoods.

But Mum wasn't worrying about Ash and Rainbow's upbringing. She was worrying about Ben and me on the Pier.

'How funny?' she asked suspiciously. 'What do you mean?'

'Unpleasant-funny,' I muttered evasively.

'They didn't *do* anything, Jo?' she insisted.

'No, course not.'

'You said . . .'

'They were just hanging around,' I said angrily, irritated by her questions. I didn't want to talk about Ash and Rainbow. I was worried and wanted to think about how I was going to avoid them.

She was silent for a moment, gazing out of the kitchen window. 'They cried at their dad's funeral,' she said vaguely. 'Wouldn't stop. I suppose we should feel sorry for them. They were only children. But they are a bit much, even for growing up round here.'

'I don't feel sorry for them,' I said flatly.

I was watching for them on the streets. I had promised to meet them in the Tesco car park before midnight, but it was a promise I had no intention of keeping. I was wondering what would happen if they decided to visit. The tower block is surrounded by terraces and roads and cuts leading down to the main street and the docks. You can escape lots of ways provided you know where you're going.

'They had a car,' Ben said.

Mum's eyebrows went up. 'Again!'

She knew all about Ash and Rainbow's criminal activities. They had been caught several times already, and spent a month in community care after wrecking a brand new Fiesta. They told the magistrates they wanted to start a taxi service.

'Joy riding,' I nodded.

'You weren't in the car?' she cried in alarm.

'No, of course we weren't in the car. We just *saw* them.'

'You sure?'

'Mum!'

She relaxed, stubbing her cigarette out in the ashtray. She'd had enough stress for one day and she hadn't been to work at the Cineplex yet. By the time she finished her shifts there and the cleaning afterwards she would be exhausted. She never got home before one o'clock in the morning.

'Just because they lost their parents,' she said absent-mindedly, as if she were trying to think of a reason for going round wrecking other people's lives, or their cars.

'Maybe they've nothing else to live for,' I suggested, trying to be funny, though come to think of it, I couldn't see much else Ash and Rainbow *had* got to live for.

But Mum didn't care anyway. 'That doesn't mean they have to be criminals,' she said firmly, as if I was arguing with her. 'You understand, Jo?'

'Yes, Mum,' I agreed wearily.

I knew she was thinking about us. Half the families on the estate were without fathers, and we were just another statistic. Mum worried about it all the time, but she wouldn't tell me. She seemed to be lost inside her own head right now, going off on one of her journeys into silence. She was often like this: standing at the kitchen sink over the washing up, dreaming of a better world nobody could find. It was like talking to scented talcum powder some days, talking to our mum. As if she wasn't there. As if she'd gone out and left us to answer our own questions.

She'd been like that ever since Dad went away. Ben was four. I used to come home from school and find him asleep in front of the television. If I didn't get his tea, he starved. At bedtime, I read him stories and went to sleep beside the bunk bed if he was having nightmares. When he lost teeth, I was the tooth fairy.

31

I had to tell him about Dad working away, until he stopped asking.

I felt my eyes watering. I couldn't help it. I brushed the tears away and pretended to have a coughing fit. I was feeling guilty about the Pier, about shouting and losing my temper. That was the thing about losing your temper: you enjoyed it at the time, and then you felt sorry.

I sat down and put my arm around Ben. He didn't push me away. We watched *Jurassic Park* together.

At least the monsters there weren't real.

# Five

And I knew it wasn't finished.

Mum went off to work but I couldn't sleep. I couldn't get Rainbow and Ash out of my mind. It was Ash mainly. He terrified me. I lay in bed listening to Sinéad O'Connor. 'Nothing Compares 2 U'. I kept playing it, over and over again. I played it nearly every night. That was a world I could fly to. A dream I could dream. Sinéad O'Connor was my idea of heaven.

Ben climbed in with me, complaining about things with long necks chasing him, but he went to sleep when I turned the music off. He sleeps very lightly, disturbed by the slightest noise. My mind was still too full of Ash and Rainbow. They wouldn't go away. At two in the morning, I got up.

Mum was sitting in the kitchen, staring out of the window at the lights of shipping at the estuary. She hadn't changed out of her usherette's uniform.

She still cries sometimes, in the night, when the silence is unbearable and she thinks we are asleep. I try to comfort her, but I never do it very well.

'I miss him, Jo.'

'I'll make some tea.'

'I wake up wishing he was there.'

'I know.'

I stood at the kitchen window while the kettle steamed on the gas. I could see lights down on the commercial docks where they were unloading a freighter. A helicopter throbbed over the deserted streets and tenements. On the edge of darkness, a police car travelled slowly towards dawn, searching the lonely streets for criminals.

We drank the tea. I didn't say anything when she lit a cigarette.

'I don't know where he is,' she said hopelessly.

'No.'

I reckon that must be the hardest part, missing

somebody and not knowing where they are. I miss him, but I hate him as well. I could thump him, even if he is bigger than me.

'He might be drinking a cup of tea right now, Jo, just like us,' she smiled, rubbing her eyes, being cheerful. 'He might be thinking about us. Wondering where we are.'

Yes, he might, or he might be giving the kiss of life to some sweet foreign bimbo in Peru. I could do with the kiss of life. Or just some life. Something *living* to look forward to instead of fish fingers and Ash and Rainbow. You can't call Thrunscoe Comp living. Information Technology with ancient computers, music without electronic synthesisers. I bet my father has all the music you could ever need.

'Jo?'

'Yes.'

'Do you miss your dad?'

'Yes.'

'You say it like . . .'

'Drink your tea, Mum.'

I'm not trained for this. I'm not a social worker or a Samaritan. Don't jump: talk to Jo. Forget the pills: Jo has all the answers. I'm fourteen years old. I have

35

childish dislikes: spiders, maths, that kind of thing. I'm just not equipped for my mum's tears and there's nobody around to help me.

'Go to bed, Mum.'

'In a minute.'

'Go to bed.'

'*I* should be telling *you*,' she said with a tired smile.

Yes. She should. Only she isn't.

Nothing compares to you.

I miss my dad.

# Six

They were waiting for us at the school gates. Rainbow was sitting on the brick wall beside the gates, Ash was lounging on the grass, drinking Heineken. Half a dozen older kids were with them. Rainbow and Ash rarely came to school, and when they did they always got thrown out. They had been suspended more days than there were in the school year.

I felt my stomach churning.

'Why don't we bunk off?' Ben asked, his voice dry and nervous. 'Nobody will miss us. We could run now.'

'You get suspended for bunking off,' I answered. 'Mum's already upset about the cigarettes. We don't want any more trouble.'

We reached the gates.

'It's Jo,' Rainbow shouted with a big grin.

'I'm in a hurry,' I said bravely. I had to sound tough. I had to walk straight through them or they would be with us forever. There are some troubles that just won't go away.

Rainbow looked disappointed. He lumbered down off the wall and stood in front of me, grinning awkwardly. 'Just being friendly, Jo,' he said, punching my arm.

I could see his fillings. I nearly felt sorry for him, then I smelled his breath, a stale concoction of curry, beer and tobacco which made me feel sick. I had to grit my teeth not to flinch. Just my luck, being fancied by a feller whose breath smells like elephant dung.

'Right,' I muttered, trying to turn away before he noticed my grimace.

Ash got up from the grass and yawned casually, a lethal animal preparing for the kill. A crowd of older kids watched us from behind the gates. The younger kids had fled inside already. A teacher drove past in her car, studiously ignoring us. I could feel Ben trembling when I touched his arm.

'It's all right, Ben,' I said.

'Is it?' Ben whispered.

Ash came close. His grey hair looked ancient in the bright morning sunlight. 'You look colourful this morning,' he said.

I was wearing my patched jeans and a jumper stitched together out of three old ones by my mother on long winter nights. I was sometimes tempted to steal clothes from the market just to stop my mother making me any.

'Jo's amazing technicoloured jumper,' Ash said wittily.

'Yeh, right,' Rainbow agreed, nodding vigorously. 'Jo's amazing technicoloured jumper. Yeh.' He went on nodding, but a frown slowly creased his forehead. He stopped nodding and glanced at his brother. 'What's that then, Ash?'

'You know, the musical?'

'Nah,' Rainbow said, still frowning, trying to think, then shaking his massive head in admiration, amazed by his brother's general knowledge. 'What musical?'

Ash looked defeated, then shrugged. 'Fairy story or summat,' he said with a sniff. 'You like fairy stories, Jo?'

'I'm late for IT,' I said, trying to keep calm.

Ash nodded solemnly. 'You make a habit of being late, Jo?'

'No.'

'Yeh, I reckon. You were late last night.'

'The late Jo,' Rainbow grinned.

'Very late.'

They both laughed, like demented lovers on *Blind Date*. I could feel Ash's cold breath on my face. He made my skin crawl. Rainbow simply frightened me, but there was something truly awful and incomprehensible about Ash.

'I wasn't late,' I said. 'I didn't want to come.'

A car drove up to the gates and slowed down. It was the peripatetic clarinet teacher. I said a prayer under my breath. She wound down her window and smiled cheerfully at Ash and Rainbow. She was an artist, and seemed to appreciate anything out of the ordinary.

'Aren't you boys coming in?' she asked.

'Eventually,' Ash grimaced, his eyes cold with anger at her nerve, asking him questions. He smiled as if he resented her being alive.

'I do love your hair, Rainbow,' the teacher went on blithely.

'Yeh?'

'Now get inside, will you?'

'Yeh,' Ash nodded again, and watched her drive away, dumb insolence in an extremely bad mood. There was a flat evil threat in Ash's watchful eyes, like a hound scenting an escaped prisoner.

'So,' he resumed, turning his attention back to me. 'What are we going to do about you, Jo?'

'Nothing?' I suggested hopefully.

Rainbow giggled. 'Nothing,' he repeated, as if it was the funniest thing he had ever heard.

'Right,' Ash nodded theatrically, playing his part. 'Got it.'

'We have to go now,' I said.

'You do?' Ash smiled.

I was holding Ben's arm. 'Yes.' I started to pull him away. But Ash wasn't ready for the end of the game.

'Not the gawk,' he said curtly.

Ben pulled his arm free. 'I told you,' he shouted indignantly. 'I'm not a gawk.'

But Ash wasn't listening. 'The gawk has to get a hair cut,' he went on, ignoring Ben. 'His hair is too long. Not the fashion, Jo. Not suitable for Ratspit

41

Comp. Letting the team down. That right, Rainbow?'

'Yeh.'

'Cut the gawk's golden locks.'

'Wot?' Rainbow asked, confused.

'Golden locks.'

'It's blond, 'en it?'

'You touch my brother, and I'll kill you,' I said. I don't believe it, but I said it.

We were alone at the gates now. The audience had dissolved. The clarinet teacher was getting out of her car. She locked the doors and stared back towards the gates. The teachers parked their cars behind a high security fence. She padlocked the gates and started walking back down the drive towards us. There are angels. There is justice. She was frowning.

Ash saw her. 'Fairy story,' he said under his breath in frank disbelief.

Rainbow gawped at the clarinet teacher. His tiny mind couldn't process the information: she was coming back.

Ash and Rainbow sauntered away down the road. They weren't going to bother. They had plenty of time and being suspended from school again wouldn't make much difference to them. They had all the time in my world.

'Scissors,' I heard a harsh voice calling down the road in the cold October morning air. 'Scissors.'

'They won't, will they?' Ben asked urgently, looking up at me.

'Won't what, Ben?'

'Cut my hair.'

'Over my dead body,' I managed to say with a smile.

What a joker.

# Seven

At the end of the day, Ben disappeared.

We always met after school. Sometimes we went on our bikes along the promenade. Sometimes we visited the shopping precinct with friends and looked at the CDs we couldn't afford. If we had any cash, we went to McDonald's and feasted on junk food. I love junk food. Ben worships it. The happiest day of our lives was the day I bought Sinéad O'Connor's first album and we went for a double helping of cheeseburgers and french fries and hot apple pie with ice cream. In our wildest after-school dreams, that was the kind of thing we would do every night, when we won the lottery *and* the Grand National.

But tonight, Ben wasn't waiting for me at the school gates.

I knew straight away. I'd told him during lunch break to make sure and meet me at the gates. We had to stick together, then at least neither of us would get caught walking home alone. But he wasn't there.

I ran to the staffroom. The staff were slumped in tatty armchairs, smoking, drinking black coffee, defeated.

'What is it, Jo?' Mr Godwin the gym teacher asked me briskly.

'It's my brother,' I gasped. 'He's gone.'

'He is eleven,' Mr Vaughan yawned from behind the *Guardian.*

'But he never goes without me,' I said urgently.

'Maybe you should let him.'

The clarinet teacher smiled at me sweetly. 'Maybe he's on his way home already, Jo.'

'No.'

'He's a good boy, he wouldn't do anything wrong.'

I stared at her in amazement. Didn't she understand? It wasn't what Ben might do that worried me – it was what Ash and Rainbow might do to him. 'It's not Ben I'm worried about,' I said.

'I thought you were?'

'No, I mean . . .'

Mr Taplin the geography teacher swallowed a giant mouthful of smoke, choked, went bright red, then lit another cigarette.

'Go home, Jo.'

'You saw them, Miss,' I said urgently, trying to keep the clarinet teacher's attention, but her attention had already drained out of the room. It was late afternoon. She was exhausted. She smiled at me weakly. 'You saw Ash and Rainbow, didn't you? You know what they're like.'

A shudder travelled round the staffroom. Three teachers got up and left. The clarinet teacher went pale.

'What a pair,' she sighed.

'They've got my brother,' I shouted. There was a stiffening in the tobacco drenched air. 'Don't you understand!'

'Calm down, Jo.'

'They've got Ben.'

'Nobody . . .'

I was gone.

I raced down the corridor and past the Head's

office. I slammed the main doors back hard so that they vibrated against the jamb. I grabbed my bike and shot up the drive. There was nobody about. The grounds were deserted. Every afternoon, school emptied faster than a football ground after a riot. I drove down on the pedals and grit flew up off the road. I was out of the gates and swerving through traffic faster than an ambulance on an emergency call-out.

Ben wasn't at home. I knew that without climbing all the way up several hundred concrete steps to find out, but the vacant flat stunned me like a surprise blow to the head. I sat down on a chair and stared out of the windows. The estuary shone blue in autumn sunlight. It was a cold, clear day and you could see for miles – but you couldn't see Ben. I couldn't, anyway. I stared out of the window as if I hoped that if I looked long enough Ben would come into view.

Ben was with Ash and Rainbow.

I searched the estate for an hour. I rode round in frantic circles like the victim in some terrifying computer game. I shouted his name on street corners. I checked the shops where he might be buying sweets. I knew I wasn't going to find him but what else could

I do? Where else could I go: to the police? my mum? The police would just say wait a few hours, but Mum would go ballistic if I told her Ben was missing. Us going missing is one of her worst nightmares. I think my dad started them. I could only be grateful she was working afternoons and nights, getting a double dose of *Texas Chainsaw Massacre*. I went back to the empty flat several times but Ben was never there. Night was closing in. I left a note for Mum saying we were doing homework round at a friends. We hadn't got any friends who did homework but she didn't know that. Then I went back out into the darkness to continue my search.

The streets were dreary and badly lit, full of cold shadows that seemed to hide all the horrors you could imagine. I went down to the docks but the security guards wouldn't let me through the gates in case I wrote graffiti on the walls or stowed away on a boat. I became more and more depressed: nobody cares about my brother, nobody cares about me, I got the front door key the day I was born. That kind of thing. I felt waves of self-pity carrying me out into some sea I couldn't control. I thought again about the police, but people on our estate never go to the police for help. I even thought about telephoning the music teacher but I couldn't find her number. All the teachers at our school are ex-directory. They get fed up with the midnight calls and threats of kidnap and violence. And anyway, what use had the clarinet teacher been when I told her Ben had gone missing? What use were any teachers?

I was standing outside the estate's derelict social club when I saw them. In an Escort. Spitting smoke and sparks from the exhaust and wheels and crashing into dustbins. I heard the dustbins crunching and saw Ben on the back seat of the Escort, waving his arms around in excitement, or terror, it was difficult to tell at such a distance. Ash and Rainbow were in the front seats.

I leaped on my bike and tore after them.

The Escort braked round a corner and I heard the gears being pulverised. I stood up on the pedals. I took the corner as the Escort reversed into another row of dustbins and Ben's face appeared in the rear window, beaming at me like a maniac. Was he drunk? Had they been giving him something to drink? He waved again, and appeared to laugh when the edge of the rear bumper smashed into the dustbins, sending a cacophony of tin music up to the flats. Then the Escort crashed through first-second-third gears in split seconds and we were racing; the ugly brothers in the lead, me like an idiot trying to keep up on a second-hand mountain bike.

The chase went on for an hour. They teased me. They speeded up and slowed down. Whenever I thought I'd lost them, they would turn up again. They shot through red lights. They mounted pavements and bounced into lampposts. At one dangerous moment, I thought they were going to skid straight into M & S for a chicken tikka sandwich. They drove splendidly, I had to admit that, and only dented the car when they wanted to. And all the time, Ben waved and encouraged me from the rear window, bouncing up and down on his seat, Ash and Rainbow's biggest fan. I could have killed him myself.

My only hope in this nightmare was that they wouldn't end up crashing. Or getting caught. That was one thing I didn't want to have to explain to Mum.

After an exhausting hour, they headed back towards the estate, and we did a final lap round the tower blocks. Twockers always prefer the estates. They like to be seen by their friends and admirers. They enjoy the recognition. Being seen is the entire point.

I was dying. I only smoked one cigarette a day, but my lungs were charcoal. At the end of the longest hour of my life, I knew I couldn't pedal another metre.

I gave up.

And Ash and Rainbow revved the engine, dipped their lights in taunting recognition, and drove away into the darkness of night where they could do anything they liked to my innocent brother, because nobody would see.

# Eight

I went home defeated.

Mum would be back from the Cineplex soon. It was gone midnight. She would be tired. Drained. Suffering her Friday-night blues after the chainsaws and the back-row couples trying to undress each other in the trailers. She would murder me when she learned the truth about Ben. With her bare hands. Nothing sissy like a chainsaw.

I wheeled my bike into the lightless entrance and pressed the button for the lift. You live in hope. The door opened. A whiff of curry and chips blasted me backwards but I was used to that. I've been living here all my life. A couple were kissing amid the crisps and lottery tickets and glue bottles. I didn't even want to take my bike into that mess, but I hadn't the leg-energy to walk up the stairs and the lifts don't work all that often.

I heard the hissing of the machinery as we rose to heaven. The lovers were already there, apparently, though they might have been having an epileptic fit, it was hard to tell. I kept my eyes closed and rested my mind, listening to their overture. I vow I'll never fall in love, not if it involves all that effort. You'd be less tired working nights in the fish fingers factory.

We thumped to a halt and the automatic doors opened: a night for miracles.

I walked along the corridor. Rubbish sailed past me in the night, somebody too tired to carry their bin down. The chute hasn't been emptied for months. Rats bite you if you try to clear it.

Ben was in the kitchen. He was crying.

When I opened the door and pushed my bike inside, he was in darkness, but I could hear him crying. I dumped the bike and went straight to him. I put my arms round him. 'They hurt you?'

'No, Jo.'

'You sure they didn't hurt you?'

53

'I'm all right.'

I could hear the muffled words, the tears. His head was buried in my shoulder. I went on hugging him.

'I'll kill them.'

'Jo!'

'I don't care.' I was always telling Ben violence didn't work out. 'Killing's OK, in the cirumstances,' I said.

'They didn't hurt me.' He dried his eyes and blew his nose. In the darkness, I could hear the pain. Something was definitely wrong. I turned the light on and casually filled the kettle.

'Mum will be home soon,' I said.

'Yes.'

'Let me look at you.' I looked him up and down. He was all right. There was no sign of bruises or blood. He was wearing his own clothes and still had his hair. They hadn't carried out their threat to cut it. 'Do I need to know anything?' I asked.

'Yes.'

I took a deep breath. 'Right. OK.'

I let the kettle boil and made two cups of tea. Ben never moved. He was breathing hard which he always does when he is frightened. I went quickly through various terrible alternatives but couldn't think of one that seemed likely. We stayed in the kitchen, drinking our tea. The sounds of a fight drifted down the landings, then a woman's voice screaming abuse, and a door slamming. Funeral music.

'I can turn the light out,' I said, thinking he might prefer the dark.

'No.'

'If it helps.'

'It won't.' He put his hand in his coat pocket and handed me a brown envelope.

I opened the envelope. There was no letter. Just some photographs, Polaroids, taken without a flash, but clear enough to identify Ben's excited smile. I flicked through the pictures. Mum would be pleased. She would be over the moon.

The pictures were all of Ben twocking an Escort. The Escort's number plate was clearly displayed. He looked proud in the pictures. He had a screwdriver in his hand to wreck the central locking system. His hand was already inside the car. He looked pleased as Punch. He was grinning for the camera.

Ash and Rainbow were nowhere to be seen. Naturally.

If the police got hold of these, Ben would be in serious trouble. Mum would go wild. And if Ben told the police about Ash and Rainbow, *they* would go wild.

'What did they do with the car?' I asked, as if I couldn't guess. I knew the twockers' favourite game. Burning other people's cars.

But they hadn't burned the Escort.

'They drove it somewhere,' Ben said quietly.

I could hear high heels clattering along the corridor, like commas in a life sentence. It was Mum coming home from the Cineplex. She would take one look at Ben and know something was wrong.

'Where did they drive it, Ben?'

He blushed: blue eyes, pink cheeks, blond curls, innocent smile. Ash and Rainbow would have to wreck that innocent smile. They couldn't tolerate innocence, not running free on this estate.

I heard the key turning in the lock.

'The police station,' Ben said in a whisper. 'They parked it in front of the police station.'

I might have known.

'Go,' I whispered urgently, pushing Ben out of the kitchen as the door opened. 'Get to bed.'

'Hello, Jo,' Mum shouted, cheerful for the first Friday night in months. 'I got us some chips.'

# Nine

I couldn't sleep. My mind was racing with pictures of Ash and Rainbow, and Ben waving from the back of a car. I saw blue lights every time I closed my eyes, and heard sirens wailing in the streets. I kept thinking about what might have happened, what could have gone wrong, and the horrors kept me wide awake. I thought the night was never going to end.

Getting out of bed, I stood at the window for a long time, listening to the night silence. The lights at the estuary always made me feel safe. I could dream all sorts of dreams when I was watching the estuary: ships leaving and returning; tides turning with the moon. The estuary was always changing, but it was always the same. I think that is what I liked.

Then with a jolt, I heard the letterbox rattle. There had been no sound from the lift. Somebody must have come up the stairs. I ran to the door and opened it. The corridor was in darkness. I heard a scuffle on the stairs and then feet echoing down the concrete steps. In the darkness, a metal door clanged, then there was silence. I closed the door and picked the envelope up. Another brown envelope, the same kind as the one containing the Polaroids. I went back to my room and turned the lamp on.

There was a single sheet of paper.

*Access your e-mail*, the scrawled message told me.

I stared at the words. They were written in black biro. The paper was torn from a school homework book. The words had been scored deep into the page.

I hadn't accessed my e-mail for days. It cost money, and we hadn't much, and nobody ever wrote to me anyway. I was on the Internet because Mum won a grand prize at Bingo and she wanted us to have something educational. We got an Apple-Mac. It was part of a deal when one of the fish processing factories replaced their computers: Apple-Macs started appearing all over town with special offers. Ours had a built-in modem.

I stared at the screen. I could see my face, leering at me in the light of the lamp. I looked like a ghost, peering from the other side of reality.

I knew the scrawled message was from Ash and Rainbow. But why did they want me to access my e-mail? And where had they got my e-mail address from?

I took a deep breath and switched the computer on. I clicked the mouse to the communications programme. I'm sinead@linnet-co-uk. You can guess who Sinéad is. I have a password from my dreams: Peru.

There was a thirty-second pause and then Linnet came back with the news: I had a message waiting for me.

But if it was from Ash and Rainbow, I still couldn't work out how they knew my e-mail address, and where they had access to a computer this late at night. I found it difficult to believe they even knew how to use a computer.

I told Linnet to download my mail. It was from school. I stared at the e-mail address:

kids@linnet-co-uk. Our school computer club.

My breathing began to relax. Somebody must have left a joke on the Internet for me. It might have been there days. It might even be from a teacher, telling me I'm brilliant.

I asked for the message. The words appeared like magic.

*Howd you lyke the fotas?* the words on the screen asked me.

My heart stopped. I couldn't breathe. Nobody at school had left this message. The spelling didn't prove it was Ash and Rainbow, because everybody in our school spelled like that just to annoy the teachers. But I guessed it was them. It had Ash's lovely ironic ring, Rainbow's brutal sense of humour.

But how had they sent it from school? They never *went* to school.

Then I knew. They were there now. They had delivered the brown envelope and then raced to the school. They were sitting there *right now*.

I began to tremble. I could feel them on the other side of town, watching me from the darkness, laughing at my surprise and fear. They were talking to me in the middle of the night.

I glanced back at the screen. I finished reading the message.

*The rest are even better,* it said. *Next message at three.*

The *rest*! My nightmare had begun.

I sat at the window for an hour. There was a thin light of dawn at the estuary even this late in the year. I could smell fog and seaweed and the immense yearning for travel and distance which sometimes hangs on the air, the timeless dreams of people for escape. I wanted to wake my mum, but couldn't bear to bring any more trouble into her life. I couldn't even tell Ben. I was alone.

At three o'clock, I accessed my e-mail again.

*bi bi JoJo,* the computer teased as the Victorian clock down on the commercial docks chimed three. *See you at four.*

I jumped up from the computer and swore. I felt like getting my bike and crossing town to the school. I would have gone straight for them, I was so mad. And I was exhausted. I could hardly stand. I sat down at the computer and drifted into a strange trance, then hurt my back, jerking awake as I slipped out of the chair. I went to bed and lay down.

I had trouble sleeping after that. I don't know whether I was dreaming, but I heard footsteps in the corridor, and then a dog barking frantically, and then a sickening thud. I would have got up to have a look but I couldn't bring myself to move. I lay in the neon darkness listening to police sirens and silence more noisy than a rock concert. I drifted out to the estuary on an oil tanker where I must have gone to sleep.

Then it was time to return to the screen. It was four o'clock in the morning.

*Blakmale,* the last message from Rainbow and Ash announced, as if I couldn't guess. *Leanne: Monday morning.*

Leanne was Ash's girlfriend.

And the birds along the foreshore were going crazy, singing their dawn anthem: *see you at skool.*

It was going to be a long weekend.

# Ten

The weekend seemed to last forever, but I was hardly longing for it to end. I didn't tell Ben what had happened on Friday night. He was worried enough already. We burned the photographs in a building-site brazier on our way to school. I told him everything was all right.

The police cars were just leaving when we arrived at school. There were two of them this morning. The police often got called out overnight: people on the estate complaining about vandalism or kids spraying graffiti. We watched them go, blue lights flashing for no reason, showing off. Ben always got excited when he heard the sirens. He imitated their wail, waving as they went past. The headmaster was in the drive, watching them, talking to the caretaker.

I went straight to the bicycle sheds. Ben trailed behind. Leanne was nearly always in the sheds first thing in the morning, having a smoke, chatting with her friends. This morning, she was waiting for me. She was leaning against the wire fencing, smoking and staring at the sky. Her blue eyes were misty and vacant. She had a tiny white scar on her chin, and thick black hair, parted in the middle and stiff with gel. I wanted my hair like that, short at the back and falling like a curtain down to my chin. I used to imagine finding Leanne in the bicycle sheds, the most envied girl in the whole school, my best friend, waiting just for me. But I knew this morning wasn't going to be the kind of dream I had had in mind.

She nodded after the police cars.

'You see them?'

'Yeh.'

'They reckon somebody broke into the computer rooms,' she yawned. 'Messed around with the computers.'

'No,' I said ironically. 'Who'd do a thing like that?'

Leanne smiled. She watched me for a second, and then stubbed her cigarette out on the ground. 'Did you get the messages?' she asked, her voice croaky and bored. She was famous for looking bored. Whenever she got told off, she yawned. She had been expelled for smoking in science classes and wearing black lipstick in assembly. The only time she ever got upset was if you asked her about the accident that had given her the tiny white scar. Ash had been driving when that happened. She never talked about it. 'Well?' she said impatiently.

'Yes,' I managed to reply, locking my bike and giving Ben a push. I was having difficulty keeping control of my voice. Ben didn't move and I pushed him again.

'What?'

'See you inside.'

'I don't want to go inside.'

'Go. I want to talk to Leanne.'

I didn't want Ben to know about the messages on the Internet. I didn't want him involved in Ash and Rainbow's painful plans, whatever they were going to be. Ash and Rainbow were my business. I glanced at Leanne. She yawned and lit another cigarette.

'You go out with Ash,' Ben told her cheerfully, as if the information would come as a complete surprise to her.

Leanne blinked. She managed to yawn and look astonished at the same time. 'That's right,' she nodded.

'Why?'

'Ben!'

Leanne blinked again. She seemed puzzled by Ben's sweet smile. She watched him vaguely through a cloud of smoke. 'He's a lovely feller,' she said suddenly, deciding to humour Ben, frowning into the sunlight. 'When you know him.'

'Oh.'

'And I like his grey hair. I think it's distinguished.'

'Oh,' Ben said again, apparently considering this.

'Ben,' I muttered, but he was already going. Even Ben couldn't stand too much excitement, and I had never heard Leanne say so much.

She stared at me when we were alone. 'He's dead weird, your brother,' she said flatly.

'No, he isn't.'

'You want to look after him.'

'Why *do* you go out with Ash?' I asked abruptly.

67

I thought perhaps if I could find out what was attractive about Ash to a girl I might discover where he was vulnerable. There must be something sensitive and vulnerable about him, even if he did appear to be switched off most of the time.

Leanne blinked like an android in danger of getting out of control. She stubbed her cigarette out with her DM boots and glared at me. She must waste a fortune on half-smoked cigarettes, and she only smoked the most expensive.

'Ash said you were stupid,' she snarled.

'Thanks.'

'I go out with him because he's the best.'

'Right.'

'The best, see. Despite what people say. You don't know anything about him.'

'OK!' I protested. 'I'm sorry I asked.'

Leanne took a deep breath and went on glaring at me, challenging me to speak. I didn't.

'I got a message for you,' she said finally. 'OK?'

'OK.'

'He can't come to school today.'

'He never comes to school.'

'Waste of time, ent it?'

'You're here.'

'You going to listen, Jo, or just keep talking until your time's run out altogether? Permanent! I don't mind, really I don't. I couldn't care less. Only this is boring.'

'Sorry.'

'You ready to listen?'

'Yes.'

'Ash said to ask you, did you like the film?'

'Yes.'

She meant the photographs.

'Family album,' she said with a tight hard laugh.

'I understand.'

'Your little brother twocking . . .'

'I know what was in the photographs!' I shouted, getting angry, forgetting who I was talking to: Leanne, the girl who went out with Ash.

Leanne went white. She was nervous, or angry. She wasn't used to people speaking to her like that. Unless they were Ash.

'I got to say what he told me,' she said in a breathless croak.

'Is that right?'

'He said to tell you the rest of the Polaroids are

on their way to the cops, unless you meet him tonight.'

'How many more did they take?' I asked.

'Don't waste time, Jo. They go to the police, unless you meet them tonight. That's the dare. Maybe they will, maybe they won't. I wouldn't know. It's up to you to take the risk, or meet them like they say.'

I felt faint. 'Where?' I asked.

'The high-rise. Orwell Street.'

'What time?'

'He just said be there.'

'Great.'

'You'll have to wait.'

'How long?'

She shrugged and dropped her cigarette to the floor, stubbing it out among the little pile she had already created.

She walked off without another word. The bells were ringing for assembly. The thing I don't understand about Leanne is that she is beautiful and intelligent. She has dead-fashionable black hair and a thin white face with high cheekbones and dramatic make-up, but she also has a brain like a razor blade. She just never uses it. She once won a Mensa medallion for answering questions and never recovered from the derision of her family and friends. 'Who do you think you are?' her mother laughed at her. 'Wot's Mensa?' her brother sneered. She can answer questions *and* break hearts. Why does someone like that go out with someone like Ash?

I walked after her.

# Eleven

They didn't keep me waiting long. The high-rise is down by the docks and empty most nights except for the pub and club trade. Gangs used to hold fights on the top levels until they found more dangerous places to have fun – like motorway flyovers. You would have to be insane or very tough to leave your car parked there overnight.

Rainbow and Ash arrived together, walking slowly out of the wintry darkness. Leanne was in the shadows behind them, her cigarette glowing redly.

'Nice to see you, Jo,' Ash shouted from the far end of the empty high-rise. 'Glad you could come.'

In the eerie quiet, I could hear the sea booming

against the shores, and Ash's voice echoing hollowly backwards and forwards between the shadowy pillars of the car park. As they walked, Rainbow started whistling music from a spaghetti western. They walked like a pair of gunfighters down a deserted western street.

'*A Fistful of Dollars*,' Rainbow said with a wild laugh.

'*High Plains Drifter*,' Ash said with his ironic smile.

I wondered why they had picked this particular high-rise. The kind of blokes who parked their cars here at night were dangerous to know: drunkards and casino boys, hungry boxers eager to take their Indian take-aways home. It was the sort of place the police never visited. I guessed the risk element excited Ash's sense of humour.

They stopped in front of me.

'Ever black-boxed a vehicle, Jo?' Ash asked after a pause.

'No.'

'You know much about cars?'

'Nothing.' I was lying. I had driven an old transit van on rough ground last summer when Mum had a job on a farm, helping with the pea-picking. I was supposed to be giving her a hand but the farmer only paid 50p an hour and I got sunstroke. Then I found the old transit van. The keys were still in the ignition. It had been abandoned and there were weeds growing through the floorboards but the engine still worked and I spent hours learning how to drive across rutted fields and through overgrown woods, the perfect preparation for driving around town. By the end of the summer I could drive. But I didn't want Ash and Rainbow to know that I could. Ignorance is a lot safer than information on our estate.

Rainbow already looked stunned. Everybody knew about cars. He stared at me with fresh interest, as if I was an alien from some weird planet where they hadn't progressed to motorised vehicles.

Ash glanced around the vast dark spaces. He never looked surprised. It was part of his tough image. I could have said I was Liam Gallagher and he wouldn't have blinked an eye. He was only interested in machines. And there weren't many machines in the high-rise car park to interest him.

'Astra, Escort, Metro, that's what we want,' he said, explaining his trade. 'You see any of those, Jo?'

I looked around. I wasn't very good at cars, but I could see a Metro down at the far end of the level. I nodded in that direction, and we walked towards it. The floor was slippery with water and pools of oil. The Metro was parked by a flight of concrete stairs. It was bright yellow.

'Why did I mention the Astra, the Escort, and the Metro, Jo?' Ash asked me as we walked, like a driving instructor meeting a pupil for the first time.

'I don't know.'

'Blimey,' Rainbow grunted.

'Easy to start,' Ash explained patiently.

We stopped by the concrete stairs. Leanne leaned against one of the pillars. I noticed the way Rainbow kept his eyes on the entrance, listening for the sound of footsteps, while Ash admired the yellow Metro, touching its delicate paint, checking the tyres. The Metro was like a field of buttercups on the edge of a volcano. The radio aerial was unbent. The bumpers were shiny and black. It was brand new.

'You know why yellow is the best colour?' Ash asked in a whisper.

'You can't miss it?' I guessed.

They both applauded. Even Leanne looked

pleased, as if I was doing a test she wanted me to pass.

'That's right, sunshine,' Ash beamed. 'You can't miss it, not unless you actually *want* to miss it.' He smirked at the very idea. Nobody in their right mind would want to miss the chance of wrecking a car. 'Easy to see,' he went on. 'Stands out in a crowd. Let's have a look now.'

He walked round the car examining every inch of paintwork. I followed him, pushed along by Rainbow. Leanne watched us, smoking one of her endless cigarettes. There were no dents on the car. No scratches. No signs of damage to the paintwork. Ash glowed with pleasure.

'Beautiful,' he said with a triumphant smile.

He took a heavy hammer from his pocket, pointed to the driver's window, and then smashed it before I could speak. The movement was so quick I jumped back nervously into Rainbow's waiting arms. He caught me and held me close for several seconds. I shivered; I could feel his heart beating.

'All right, Jo?' he whispered against my ear. I remembered he fancied me. I still didn't like the idea. I nodded, trying to relax. I was trembling. Apart from anything else, I was sure the noise of breaking glass would raise the dead. 'It'll be all right,' Rainbow told me.

And nothing happened. The sound echoed up and down the high-rise as we listened but nobody came, nobody heard the breaking glass. When it stopped, Rainbow let me go. Then Ash reached inside the car and opened the door.

'You need a screwdriver with central locking,' he explained, climbing into the front seat and reaching across to unlock the passenger door. He had a pencil torch between his teeth. 'You also need something sharp in case there's a Krooklock fitted. You can cut through them with wire cutters.'

'Scissors,' Rainbow joked happily.

'But not on this model,' Ash went on with a professional smile, like a salesman talking to a school of car thieves. 'You watching, Jo?'

I nodded.

With a yank, Ash jerked the steering wheel to release the steering lock. 'There,' he sighed, as if he had broken into the Bank of England.

Rainbow stood at my side, watching. His expression seemed to be full of delight and admiration.

This was his brother twocking a car. I could feel the pressure of his watchful violence close to my shoulder.

But I could also feel Leanne. She had left the pillar where she had been leaning. She was keeping close, watching over Rainbow's shoulder. When I glanced at her, she nearly smiled.

'If the steering lock isn't on, you got to put it on and *then* break it,' Rainbow explained cheerfully.

'Why?' I asked, not really interested, listening for the approach of the law, or a couple of heavy-weight drunks in love with their yellow Metro.

'Because if you don't,' Leanne said before Rainbow could speak, 'the car will automatically lock as soon as it moves.' There was a pause. I glanced from the brothers to Leanne. So she knew all about black-boxing. I watched her, interested, trying to work it out, then Ash and Rainbow both smiled, pleased, enjoying themselves.

'You can listen to Leanne, Jo,' Rainbow said proudly. 'We taught her everything she knows. She's the best.'

'Right,' I said. 'OK. Why will the car lock when it moves, Leanne?'

Rainbow snorted his disbelief. He couldn't believe

I was so ignorant. He sighed impatiently, but Ash touched his arm, restraining him. He nodded towards Leanne.

'Because it automatically locks if you aren't starting it normally,' Leanne explained casually, as if she was trying to tell me how to use a new computer game.

'With the ignition key?'

'That's right,' she said.

'That's the truth,' Rainbow nodded, sounding bored.

In the Metro, Ash was fiddling around underneath the steering column. He held the pencil torch between his teeth and told me to come closer. I kneeled down and watched. He jerked at the column underneath the steering wheel and pulled away the flap hiding the ignition box. I could see a mass of wires coiled tightly together.

'The Metro has a switch to bypass the ignition key,' Ash told me, using the torch to show me inside. 'Other cars, you got to join two wires together to get started. No bother, either way.' He pressed the switch and the Metro stuttered into life. 'Get in,' Ash said, opening the passenger door.

I climbed into the back and Leanne followed me. Rainbow sat in the front with his brother. The engine gunned in the darkness. Ash didn't use the headlights. He pulled the choke right out and then let the engine roar. We sounded like a jumbo jet in a matchbox. I felt my pulse beating rapidly. I wanted to get away. I wanted to be out of there before the owner of the Metro returned and saw us twocking his precious car.

But to my amazement, I also felt excited. 'Let's go,' I whispered under my breath, but Leanne heard me. She half-turned and stared at me, then looked away. She lit a cigarette but didn't offer me the packet. I would have been too excited to smoke anyway.

We reversed the length of the high-rise floor and I was thrown forward into the back of the passenger seat. My head thumped the headrest. With a crash of the gears, Ash put the car into first and I sprawled backwards onto the floor. I could hear Rainbow laughing, a high-pitched war cry, savage enough to unnerve a platoon of Paras.

'That was black-boxing,' Ash shouted over his shoulder.

'Yeh,' Rainbow yelled.

'Now you know how to start a car, Jo.'

'Yeh,' Rainbow bellowed.

'So let's have some speed.'

'Yeh,' Rainbow cried in an ecstasy of excitement.

'Are you ready for some speed, Jo?' Ash asked me over his shoulder.

I nearly said Yeh. But I didn't. I pushed myself into the corner of the back seat and closed my eyes. I had felt like this once before, at the top of the roller coaster in Paradise Park. No turning back, no way to escape. In Paradise Park I left the contents of my stomach behind me. Tonight, I hadn't eaten. There was only my stomach.

Then we dived.

# Twelve

Twockers like to take risks. That's the point, the meaning of the whole adventure. The speed buzz and the danger of crashing. Getting caught is just a chance you have to take, not much fun or very creditable, but part of the game. Heroes don't get arrested too often; it ruins their reputations. All you have to do is say, 'I'm still a juvenile, you can't touch me,' and you're off to do it again, but your audience has probably gone home by then. Being seen by your friends is the real triumph, the majesty of twocking. Your chance of being famous for fifteen minutes. Most of the twockers are fifteen or sixteen like Ash and Rainbow, but some of them are kids, thirteen, fourteen. The youngest in our town is ten and he clocked a dozen cars a night for weeks on end before the police caught him.

I don't know when I thought all of this. It flashed through my mind like a name that you can't quite grasp, flying out of reach. As we crashed through the barriers out of the high-rise I wasn't all that interested in the history of joy riding. I was plastered to the back seat of the Metro like spray-on leather. At my side, Leanne wedged herself into the corner. She used both hands to steady herself against the front seat.

'Divine,' Ash yelled as the Metro bounced off a retarder on the exit from the high-rise.

'Fly me to the moon,' Rainbow crooned in his terrible drone.

Ash and Rainbow leaped about inside the car as if they were on a mobile trampoline. They couldn't sit still they were so excited. I opened my eyes for several seconds and tried to remember a prayer, but praying didn't seem the right thing to do. Escaping seemed the right thing to do, and with Ash and Rainbow occupying the front seats, that wasn't much of an option.

'Hang on to the headrest,' Leanne shouted as I

was thrown painfully against the back of the passenger seat for a second time. My head was beginning to throb with the pain and the excitement. I grabbed the back of the seat and tried to see where we were going.

We raced through the heart of town and then did a screaming u-turn in the middle of the road, coming back along the same road but on the wrong side. It might have been dangerous if there had been any traffic, but we only terrified a couple of bus drivers and a container lorry. Ash would have been at home anywhere in the world, he didn't mind which side of the road he drove on.

'Ash is God,' Rainbow was gibbering in the front seat.

'The Devil,' Ash yelled, gunning the Metro through an empty petrol station, bouncing her rear end off one of the pumps. I ducked. Would a petrol pump explode after a thump like that? It didn't. The man in the office leaned out, yelling and waving his fists, but when Ash spun round and did a repeat run the man hid down beneath the till and reinforced glass windows. We hit the petrol pump again and then we were off, heading back for the bright lights of town.

'This is fun,' Ash said solemnly, steering with

casual ease like a child born in a dodgem car.

'Fun,' Rainbow grinned. 'Fun.'

The trouble was, I was beginning to believe them.

Then we turned left into the police station car park. Dozens of police vehicles were lined up in the car park. Security lights blazed out of the darkness. We went slamming into cars the whole length of the car park and I could see faces at the police station windows. A siren went off. Voices boomed over tannoys. There were lights blazing everywhere. I thought some of them must be inside the car, flashing and dazzling. I couldn't see what was happening. Ash yelled with excitement and turned the Metro on two wheels, careering back down the row of vehicles and bouncing into several of them with a delicate touch of the steering wheel. More lights blinded me. We were driving unarmed into the middle of the enemy camp.

We were gone before the cops had any idea what was happening. Nobody in their right mind would drive into a police car park and wreck a dozen cars. The police were too shocked to take action. They watched us in disbelief and by the time belief shuffled over the horizon we were gone, roaring out of town towards the motorway and darkness. From the rear seat, I watched to see if there were any blue lights following us, but there was nothing.

And then suddenly a single headlight beamed after us. Leanne turned to look. 'Motorcycle,' she said quickly to Ash.

I saw Ash glancing in his mirror. His eyes were shining. His fingers clenched the steering wheel. I watched the headlight getting closer. I could hear the engine and the wail of the siren.

'Take a left,' Rainbow yelled.

Ash swerved off the main road and we were racing behind some tall buildings, offices and deserted warehouses. The headlight was gone for a second and then back behind us.

'The railway bridge,' Leanne shouted. 'Then the lights.' I could see the sweat on her face, hear the harsh gasps of her breathing as she yelled at Ash. Her face was white in the beam of the motorcycle, her eyes dark with excitement. She knew exactly where we were going.

Ash did what she said. He spun the car savagely to the left and doused the lights. Then the Metro was bouncing over rough ground, cobbles or stones. I didn't know where we were. The headlight followed us and then disappeared. I saw a huge stretch of black sky above us, full of stars, and then we were in darkness, racing underneath a bridge. The roar of the engine echoed backwards and forwards, bouncing off the brick walls. Ash and Rainbow had their windows wound right down. Cold wind raced into my face.

When we were out from under the bridge we turned sharply to the right, the car nearly lifting off its wheels, and then Ash slammed the brakes on, yelling at us to hang on. The minute the car came to a halt, we were out and running.

I could hear the motorcycle's siren. Leanne was at my side, dragging at my arm. 'This way,' she gasped.

Even Leanne couldn't chain smoke and keep fit. She stumbled in the darkness and began to laugh. We were both laughing. I thought my lungs would burst into flame. Ash and Rainbow were yards in front of us, cursing as they staggered across the rubble and weeds.

We ran on until the sound of the siren was like a distant cry from the estuary. I had no idea where we were, but guessed we were somewhere near the old fishing docks. There was no traffic, only open spaces and deserted buildings. A cold wind sighed among the ruins. We collapsed on the rough ground, laughing with excitement and exhaustion.

There was no sign of the police. The Ash and Rainbow show had bewildered them.

I slumped to the ground, wondering if I would ever experience anything so exciting in my life again.

# Thirteen

After that we went to play snooker on the estate where Ash and Rainbow were born.

'It's a very skilful game,' Ash explained.

'Mastermind,' Rainbow nodded.

'You got to steal a white car and a red car, and then all the colours,' Ash went on as if the planet I came from knew even less about sport than about motor vehicles.

'I know how to play snooker,' I said angrily. I was exhausted, leaning against a shop frontage, trying to stop my legs trembling. We were at a crossroads. A few lights were on in the houses but there were no cars about. I had had more than enough excitement. I was bone tired and I wanted to go home.

Ash ignored my sullen slouch. 'This is the estate where I was born,' he said, staring around absent-mindedly. 'Few streets from here.'

I shrugged. What was I supposed to reply? I knew that already, and at the moment I had other things on my mind, such as where to run when the police arrived. Now that the excitement of the chase was over, I was convinced the police would know exactly what we were planning. They were probably watching us right now.

Ash lit a cigarette and blew the smoke up into the air. A dog barked in one of the houses. 'We had a mum and dad then,' Ash said with a brief smile. 'You remember those days, Rainbow, when we had a mum and dad?'

'Yeh, I remember,' Rainbow said uneasily, apprehensive, agitated, as if he didn't like his brother talking about the past.

'Yeh,' Ash said sadly. They stared at the moon together, like a couple of werewolves waiting for midnight.

Leanne stood a few yards away, the red glow of her cigarette flickering in the dark. She seemed lost in her own thoughts, withdrawn now that the chase was over. She didn't answer when any of us spoke to her.

'You live with your mum and dad, Jo?' Ash asked after a long silence.

'My mum,' I said. 'My dad left.'

Ash nodded. 'Yeh. They do. But you got Ben.'

I thought he was getting at me, mentioning Ben. I remembered the Polaroids, and glared briefly at Ash, but he wasn't being provocative. He looked sad, lost in his own unhappy memories.

'Yeh,' I said quietly.

The brothers Grim nodded in unison.

I thought about Ash and Rainbow's horrific childhood. Losing your parents was bad enough, but growing up with a grandma who earned a living selling stolen clothes would destroy most people's sense of right and wrong. Grandma sold second-hand clothes around the tenements. Only they weren't second-hand. They were new and they were the best you could get. She had people queuing up at her door all hours. You could order whatever you wanted: winter coats, school uniforms, the latest fashion lines. She could supply anything anywhere, same day delivery guaranteed.

The clothes she sold were supplied by a gang of kids working the shopping precincts and superstores. They called themselves the Sweepers. You had to be under sixteen to join the Sweepers, and if you were an infant you got paid more because nobody would suspect an infant of pilfering M & S underwear. Grandma called the infants her kindergarten gang. She had quite a big business going, with dozens of kids supplying designer dresses and designer jeans, DM boots and shoes. She had a catalogue in her brain like a computer. Five year-olds just starting infant school couldn't wait to join the Sweepers. They were more popular than the local football team.

Some of the busybodies on the estate said Grandma used to beat Ash and Rainbow with a belt when they failed to get her the clothes she needed for her orders, but everybody knew that wasn't the truth. Ash and Rainbow didn't need beating. By the time they were out of primary school, they were professionals. They even trained the other kids, running Grandma's nightschool for thieves. They were strict and methodical and knew everything there was to know about burglary because Grandma taught them and she was aristocracy. She learned all the tricks from some of her criminal friends, but she never got caught herself. It was a miracle she was given Ash and Rainbow to look after, but the police could never prove what she was doing and the welfare people never got involved. Ash and Rainbow passed on her wisdom, and could conceal clothes in hidden pockets faster than any shoplifter on police records. They enjoyed it. By the time they were ten, they were earning more money than most adults. They had a lot of experience stealing from clothes shops and supermarkets before they moved on to stealing alcohol from off-licences and then twocking for entertainment. A few years in prison, and they would be emperors of crime.

I jumped nervously when Ash spoke. 'This is the last bit, Jo,' he said almost kindly, watching me with his shrewd grey eyes.

We stared at each other for a moment, neither of us speaking. Rainbow was restless, prowling up and down the pavement, sniffing the air like a bloodhound, looking up at the stars.

'Let's go then,' Ash said.

'Where to?'

'You'll see. Leanne!' At Ash's call, Leanne stubbed her cigarette out in the gutter. She didn't bother to look up. She hadn't said anything since we left the car.

We walked away from the crossroads. I hunched my shoulders against the cold. My legs were still trembling, but I could manage. 'You all right?' Leanne asked when I stumbled, twisting my ankle on the edge of the pavement, but I didn't want her concern.

'When do I get the photographs?' I asked.

'When we finish,' Ash said.

'Is that going to be long? Only my mum gets back from the Cineplex soon.'

'Not long,' Rainbow said with his imperturbable grin.

The next hour was like a dream, dancing in my head. We found a white Escort parked outside a pub and black-boxed that so fast I thought I was still on the pavement when Ash braked and we were running for a red Astra. The Astra was even quicker, and then we were down outside the Bingo hall selecting cars like chocolates in a selection box. I kept a note of the colours. Ash agreed to count the Metro as yellow, and we only got stuck on pink. We ended up with a decorator's van that had been painted pink. We went through the rest of the snooker table so quickly I couldn't get my breath. I began to shout when I saw a colour we hadn't black-boxed. I was excited. I wanted to be the first to spot each colour. My pulse was going faster than the cars. By the time we got the last car we needed, a battered black Astra, I was shouting at Ash and Rainbow to wake up and play the game. They never said a word in reply.

Then it was over. Every ball on the table. Success in less than an hour, and not a sign of the police. I should have been over the moon with relief. I should have been celebrating. But I had been too busy to worry about the police. There was so much to do, so many practical things to concentrate on. One mistake could have got us caught. I had forgotten about Mum. I had forgotten Ben. For an hour, my life had been more intense and dangerous and *vivid* than in all the years before, and the time was gone before I knew what was happening.

'What now?' I asked Ash, dancing around in front of him. 'What can we do now?'

'Now?' Ash said with a harsh laugh.

'I'll drive next time,' I said. 'I'll drive.' I was like

a kid with a new computer. I couldn't wait to start the game again. I was jumping up and down with impatience, demanding that we get on and steal another car.

Ash and Rainbow watched me with amused interest. 'I thought you couldn't drive?' Ash said casually, pretending to be interested in a lorry rumbling up the main road towards the docks.

I shrugged. 'I meant . . . I didn't learn, you know, the right way . . .'

'Yeh, we know,' Rainbow grinned.

They seemed pleased. I had enjoyed their game. I had been thrilled by the whole thing. I was one of them now.

'*Well*! Come *on*!' I cried, 'Let's go and find another car.'

They still didn't answer. All three of them were watching me. There was a long silence, and then I heard my words, my ridiculous excitement. Reality dawned.

I glanced quickly at Leanne. She was watching me with a hard, interested gaze. For a second, I thought she seemed worried, but perhaps it was only the streetlight. She frowned and fixed the bored expression back on her face. She gave one of her terrific done-that-been-there yawns and glared at Ash, but I had seen the doubt in her eyes, the concern. It was Leanne's concern that stopped me in my tracks. What was I doing? Had I gone mad? I was supposed to be twocking to get the photographs of my brother back. I was doing this to save him from the police, not for my own enjoyment.

The guilt raced through my mind while Leanne watched me. She was still thinking, deciding something. Then she turned abruptly to Ash and Rainbow. 'Yes, right, well that's it then,' she said, her voice flat and tired, derisive, as if bored with the whole evening. 'Can we go home now, boys? If you've had enough fun? I'm fed up of this.'

Ash nodded his head slowly, showing he understood how she felt. Rainbow looked disappointed. I just felt grateful. I knew she'd said that for me. I came back to my senses.

I glanced at my watch. I was just going to get home in time, if the brothers Grim handed over the photographs and let me go. I couldn't believe they would do that.

But they did.

# Fourteen

'OK then,' Ash said. 'Like I promised.'

He handed me an envelope. I could feel the
Polaroids inside. I didn't even bother to check.

I was free. I felt like a newly-released prisoner,
blinking in the bright sunlight. I wanted to dance on
the grass verge. I wanted to celebrate my broken
shackles. I stuffed the envelope into my back pocket
and nodded. I almost held my hand out for a shake,
then realised how stupid that would look.

'Thanks,' I said instead.

'OK,' Ash nodded indifferently.

Rainbow looked miserable, depressed, fed up now
that the fun was over.

'It was OK,' I said, mumbling like an idiot.

'You ent bad, Jo,' Ash told me.

'OK,' Rainbow agreed.

I turned to leave them. I felt gleeful, overjoyed by my evening. I had gone twocking with the two worst nightmares in town. I could boast about this on the estate for months, maybe even years. I had taken their dare and not been scared out of my DMs.

'It's not so tough,' I told Ash, my voice coming back as I pushed the photographs safely into my back pocket.

'No?'

'Not like they say.'

'More fun than fear,' Ash nodded his agreement.

'Yes,' I laughed. 'I bet nicking clothes is much tougher.'

There was a twitch of electricity in the air. They went very still. Leanne was lighting a cigarette but she paused, holding the match halfway to her mouth. The match phuttered out.

I was thinking about their grandma the fence. I was thinking about the Sweepers and the kindergarten. Or I wasn't thinking at all.

'I bet nicking underwear and scarves is much more frightening,' I jeered.

I was relentless, unstoppable, driven mad by my night in the cars. I had lost all sense of proportion. I was Clint Eastwood in a spaghetti western, reckless with my new power, the pictures in my pocket. Rainbow was looking interested now, staring at me as if I were a rabbit in his colourful headlights. Ash was very quiet, watchful, alert. They were like a pair of stoats out on a hunting spree, sniffing their prey, and I was it.

'I bet nicking handkerchiefs for your criminal grandma puts twocking to shame,' I said with my stupid grin.

Silence.

A sense of how far I had gone slowly penetrated my mind. Their criminal grandma was gone. She was dead. I shrugged and stared down at my DMs. I still felt exhilarated, relieved to have survived the evening, but the exhilaration was rapidly draining away. I knew I had ruined everything now. I had stepped way beyond anything Ash and Rainbow were going to tolerate. I felt a sudden desperate need for a cigarette.

I saw Ash take a step towards me. He lifted his

fist. Then Leanne was saying something, grabbing at his arm, her voice urgent and pleading. I half-turned towards her, thinking she was speaking to me, but it was Ash she was shouting at. I couldn't seem to focus on the words. Her mouth was wide open, then I heard the word 'No' being yelled very loud. There seemed to be a lot of shouting going on.

I looked back at Ash, but Rainbow was looming right in front of him, blocking his way. Maybe he was going to hit me first. Maybe they were going to take turns.

I flinched, but nothing happened. Rainbow was arguing with Ash. He was laughing, trying to calm things down. I could see Ash trying to get round his brother but Rainbow dodged to the left and then to the right and Leanne was yelling at me again, telling me to run.

I heard her this time. I ran. I ran all the way home. Ash and Rainbow didn't follow. I was alone. As I started running, I could hear them arguing, their voices carrying through the deserted streets, Ash yelling angrily in the darkness, Rainbow grunting and laughing. Then I couldn't hear them anymore. I was away. Leanne and Rainbow had saved me.

The evening was over at last, and on my own I felt better all the time. I raced up the concrete stairs to the eighth floor and unlocked the door to our flat. And my luck stayed with me. Mum was not home. I could hear Ben snoring in his bedroom. The blue light of the television flickered in a corner. I went straight to the kitchen and put the kettle on. I stood at the window, looking down to the docks and the foreshore, the lights gleaming like an American city along the riverbank, the glimmer of lights out at the estuary bobbing with the turning tide. I was safe.

When the coffee was made, I turned the light on and sat at the breakfast bar. I opened the envelope. They were Polaroids, just like the others, which meant there were no negatives. These were all the evidence. Ash had kept his promise. It would be best to destroy them before Mum got home. She was late already. I got one of Mum's ashtrays and sat down at the breakfast bar in the kitchen.

I started looking through the pictures. They reminded me of my evening with the brothers Grim. I felt almost friendly towards them now. And to Leanne. It had been fun, like riding a roller coaster seems to have been fun when you're safely back on the ground and your stomach has stopped revolving.

I felt incredible.

I had never felt so *alive.*

The Polaroids reminded me of everything that had given meaning to my life for a single brilliant evening. It seemed a shame to destroy them.

Then I heard the key in the door. I would have to burn the pictures in the morning. I dived for my bedroom and pushed the envelope underneath the bed, and then went through to the kitchen to put the kettle on for Mum.

I was so thrilled with myself, I almost told her what a great evening I'd had.

But I didn't. I went to sleep that night dreaming of a yellow Metro.

# Fifteen

In the morning, I woke up happy.

Mum was standing by the bed with a tray in her hands. I could smell bacon and eggs and steaming coffee.

'What's this?' I muttered, staring at her blearily.

'What's it look like, dopey. Breakfast! Come on, I can't stand here all day holding this tray.'

I took the tray and rubbed the sleep from my eyes. I never got breakfast in bed. She smiled, sitting on the edge of the bed and lighting a cigarette. I heard the television booming in the sitting room.

'It's a treat,' she said. 'Like a holiday. I got some extra money for staying behind after *Midsummer*

*Mayhem.*' She looked happy. I could smell perfume and she was wearing lipstick. She looked young when she smiled.

I started eating the food, smiling and clearing my mind. If this was a trap I would need to be alert. You could never tell what stories the neighbours were telling. She might have heard about my joy riding adventures from one of the other usherettes if they'd rung before I woke up, and some of them were mean-minded enough to do that; bad news spreads like weeds in this town. I could hear Ben in the bathroom getting ready for school. I went on eating, enjoying the food but ready for anything.

Then I noticed the envelope on the floor beside the bed.

Mum noticed it at the same time. 'What's this?' she said, picking it up casually.

'Nothing.'

'Last time you said that it was your school report.'

I laughed. Hilarious idea. As if I would ever bring a school report home again. I reached for the envelope but she snatched it away. I stopped eating.

'It's nothing illegal is it, Jo?' she asked, frowning at me hard. 'You aren't in some kind of trouble?'

'No, Mum!'

She watched me anxiously for a moment, her eyes full of concern, all her light-heartedness gone. 'You would tell me?' she asked quietly.

'Yes.'

'You promise!'

I was weakening all the time. I almost told her. I *wanted* to tell her. We had never told each other lies. In a moment of madness, I stumbled towards the edge of the precipice. 'Read it if you like,' I said gaily, throwing safety out of the bedroom window.

But she wasn't like that. 'I will trust you if you promise, Jo,' she said quietly.

I managed a sigh of exasperation and she handed the envelope back. I dropped it beside the bed as if it really wasn't worth bothering about. I tried desperately to think of something to say, some sort of explanation. 'It's a love letter,' I said with a grin.

She snorted and tried to hide her amusement. 'Now I *know* you're up to something,' she said, giggling.

'Thanks a lot.'

'A love letter!'

'Cheers.'

She stood up good humouredly and opened the

curtains. Her mind was already busy with other things.

'I love bacon and eggs,' I said cheerfully, keeping her diverted.

'I know, love.'

'I could eat them every breakfast.'

'You know where the frying pan lives.'

For once, I almost felt as if I was living a real life, a proper life with things like bacon and eggs for breakfast. I finished my breakfast and got ready for school faster than a prisoner waking up on the morning of her release.

Ben chatted all the way to school. I'd shown him the last of the photographs. 'Will it be all right now, Jo?'

'I told you!'

'*Truly*?'

'It'll be all right. I promise.'

We dropped the second lot of photographs into the back of a refuse collection vehicle and watched the metal teeth obliterate the envelope along with all the other rubbish. 'There,' I told Ben. 'Are you satisfied now?'

He grinned at me, his lopsided mouth open. It was the first time he'd looked cheerful for days. He hadn't been sleeping properly. He still looked pale, ill, dark rings underneath his eyes, but he was smiling. It was a shock to realise how frightened he had been. Now he started talking about the morning's technology lesson and the model generator he was going to make with one of his friends.

To my surprise, Leanne was waiting for me at the bicycle sheds. She looked upset. I told Ben to leave us alone, and he cleared off. He didn't want to go, resenting being kept out of anything, but I'd warned him about hanging around when Leanne wanted to talk, and he went off without complaining. He didn't seem to notice Leanne's miserable expression.

'You take some risks,' Leanne said angrily when we were alone.

'I know . . .' I started to say, but she wasn't listening.

She was furious. She looked as if she hadn't slept all night. There were dark rings underneath her eyes and her face was white with tiredness. 'Couldn't you keep your mouth shut?' she said bitterly.

'Sorry.'

'Use a bit of sense?'

'Leanne . . .'

'You were free! You had your photographs back! They were going to let you go!'

I shrugged. I didn't need reminding how stupid I was.

Leanne sighed impatiently and stared towards the playground. 'They want to meet,' she said quietly after a pause, taking a cigarette out of her handbag and lighting it. She used three matches, striking them so hard they broke.

'To meet?' I muttered, trying to control my rising excitement. I must be losing the ability to think clearly. Why would they want to meet? Why was I excited at the very idea? I knew why they wanted to meet. I had said some very stupid things about their grandma. They probably wanted to play football with my head. Rearrange what was left of my brains. And yet all I could think about was twocking cars: the dream that they might want to go out for another night on the town.

Leanne was watching me with her cold sceptical stare, a tight smile on her lips, as if she could read my mind and see right through to what I was really thinking. 'You are an idiot,' she told me.

'What do you mean?'

'Twocking is for idiots,' she said impatiently.

'Ash goes twocking,' I pointed out, trying to sound clever.

She wasn't amused. 'Yeh,' she said. 'But you're not Ash.'

'And Rainbow . . .'

'Be quiet, Jo.' I heard the anger in her voice. I was confused. Last night she had seemed excited: she *was* excited. I saw how she was. But now she couldn't hide her derision. She wouldn't be disloyal to Ash and Rainbow, but I could see the contempt in her eyes. I stopped talking. 'They didn't like what you said,' she told me after a long silence.

'About their grandma,' I nodded.

'That's right,' Leanne sneered. 'About their grandma. What else did you think I meant?'

I felt my face going red. I was beginning to get mad. 'It wasn't so bad,' I muttered.

'Oh no!'

I glared at her angrily, my eyes smarting with tears. 'It was *true*!' I pointed out indignantly, shouting, defensive. I could have turned and walked away, like a suicide jumping off the top of a high building. But it was fear making me shout. It was anger at my own stupidity making me hit out.

But Leanne had a worse temper than me. She shut me up. 'You just listen,' she snapped, pushing her hair aside from her pale face. 'Ash is very sensitive about his grandma. He doesn't like people making snide remarks. He loved her. He thought she had a golden heart. She was a kind old lady, doing her best, trying to bring them up. Trying to earn a living. You don't expect to be left with two kids when you're old and on your own. She had arthritis and angina. Ash and Rainbow weren't the answer to her prayers. They were trouble. She was an old woman, and she didn't want two disturbed boys to look after, but she didn't say no, she did what she knew best, she stole, and she provided. They were never hungry. They always had clothes. You can't ask more than that. You can't do better even with real parents, and some of them don't bother. She looked after them, and you shouldn't have said what you did.'

I could have wept. I knew all this. I knew it last night, and yet still I let my mouth run away with itself. I couldn't resist having a go. All that jeering about M & S underwear and the antics of the Sweepers. I might never go twocking again because of that. I should have known better. And tonight, I might get a good thumping for my stupidity.

I glanced at Leanne. She was crying. I stared at her in shocked surprise, Ash and Rainbow gone from my mind, the school bell ringing far away. I saw the playground was empty, everybody gone in for assembly. We were alone. I pushed the time to the back of my mind.

'Leanne?'

She didn't seem to hear me. She took a cigarette from her bag, lighting it and taking a couple of drags, then throwing it to the ground and grinding it out with her heel. She rubbed her eyes and glared at me through her tears.

'You think it's all a game.'

'Twocking?'

'You think it's just fun.'

'So did you, last night,' I pointed out. I wasn't going to keep my mouth shut. I was never any good at doing that. 'I saw the way you were,' I told her.

'Yeh,' Leanne laughed bitterly. She shook her head in cold mockery of herself, staring across the deserted playing fields, the empty playground. 'Yeh, it was good,' she said. 'It's always good.'

I waited.

She sounded furious. She bit her lip, smiling at me suddenly, folding her arms across her chest, then she looked down at the ground. 'You know how I got this?' she said.

I had no idea what she was talking about. 'Got what?'

She flared at me instantly, her eyes angry, looking straight into mine. She pointed to the tiny white scar on her chin. '*This*,' she almost hissed.

I shrugged. It hadn't entered my mind. 'You never speak about it,' I muttered.

'I wonder why!'

'Leanne . . .' I wanted to comfort her, say something to stop the hurt, but I didn't know what to say. What *could* I say? I hardly knew her. For once, I kept my mouth shut.

Leanne watched me for a second, daring me to say anything, then stared away into the silence. 'You *know* we were twocking,' she said.

'How would I know!' I protested.

'Yeh, right.' She got a cigarette alight and smiled briefly, then offered me the packet. I took one, grateful for the harsh taste of the tobacco. 'It was stolen. Tesco

113

car park. Only, he was doing me a favour. It was raining. Pouring it down. He was taking me to the studio. You know the health studio, down Cromwell Road?'

'Yeh.'

'I was late. Some idiot pulled out of the car park and went straight into us. Threw my face into the dashboard. I wasn't wearing a seatbelt. I was in a hurry to get out. Ash drove us to the hospital and then scarpered. The police never found out he was driving. I woke up in hospital and that was that.'

She was quiet for a moment, smoking her cigarette. She swallowed the smoke, taking huge mouthfuls. The cigarette seemed to relax her. 'Ash went wild. Drinking. Going round the streets all night, looking for the car. He was going to kill the bloke but he couldn't find him. The car wasn't from this town. Ash wouldn't drive after that. Stopped taking cars for nearly a year. Then he started again. Said life wasn't worth living without it. There isn't much else, if you think about it. He'll kill himself one of these days,' she said, biting the words out. She coughed, tears coming to her eyes again. 'He's good to me . . .' she said.

'Leanne.'

'He's kind . . .' She broke off, biting the inside of her mouth. 'Stupid,' she said angrily. 'It was years ago.'

'It's not stupid. He looked after you, didn't he?'

'Yeh.' She blew her nose. 'But I know what people say about him.'

'Yeh, well, you should hear the women my mum works with down the Cineplex. They even gossip about themselves.'

She laughed then, and dried her eyes. She glanced towards the school. 'You were stupid last night, you know,' she said.

'I know.'

'Best if you meet them.'

'Yeh.'

'They won't hurt you.'

'Right.'

'Only don't go twocking.'

'I promise.'

She caught my eye, and we both burst out laughing. Then we walked in to school together.

Listening to Leanne, I knew I should never go twocking again, and yet when she told me where to meet Ash and Rainbow and the time, I couldn't help feeling excited. I walked to my classroom in delirium. Ash and Rainbow might be mad at me, but they might not want to hit a girl. That wouldn't do their tough image much good. They might think up something else to get rid of their anger, some dare to make me sorry for my words. A twocking dare to start my pulse racing. Ash and Rainbow might insist we spend another night twocking. They knew how much I'd enjoyed myself, but they might still imagine something so terrible even I wouldn't enjoy it.

And if they didn't, I still had one last chance. Because I had had an idea.

Listening to Leanne, the idea had suddenly come to me: I might be able to meet the brothers Grim and still stay in control; I might be able to go twocking again even if that was the last thing on their minds.

I banged my fists together, whispering 'Yeh!' in the corridor and making several kids jump. The dream wasn't over.

By the time I found Ben, I had it all sorted in my head. I hardly noticed the expression on Ben's face. He had seen me arguing with Leanne. He knew something was going on. He looked frightened. We walked together into assembly and went to our separate classes. I was too preoccupied to ask him if he was all right. I was too obsessed with my own thoughts to worry about my brother.

# Sixteen

They were waiting for me in the high-rise car park.

I took a bunch of flowers. 'I wanted to say sorry,' I said, pushing the flowers into Ash's hands. 'I was wrong to say what I did.'

Rainbow looked surprised, and then beamed all over his face. Ash stared at the flowers, holding them away from him as if they might conceal an unexploded bomb. 'Flowers?' he said, his eyebrows twitching.

'I thought you might put them on her grave,' I said.

Rainbow sighed. 'That's nice, Ash,' he said, looking at his brother for his reaction. Ash nodded numbly.

I glanced round for Leanne. She was nowhere in sight. 'Isn't Leanne coming?' I said quickly, trying to appear relaxed.

Rainbow shook his head. 'She don't approve of twocking,' he said with a big grin. 'She likes it, but she don't approve. Couldn't you tell?'

'Yeh.'

'You know: some girls!'

'Yeh.'

I took a deep breath, and decided to take the plunge. I had to get them while they were still softened up by the flowers. I had to make my suggestion seem like a sacrifice, something only a fool would suggest. 'Look,' I said. 'I know I ought to do something.'

Ash looked up from the flowers. He studied my face. 'About what?'

'The things I said. Nobody should say things like that. I know I can't really make it up to you . . .'

'Right,' Ash nodded thoughtfully.

'You brought the flowers,' Rainbow grunted.

'I ought to do something in recompense,' I said. 'You know, to make up for what I said,' I explained hastily. 'Something really dangerous.'

'Like what?'

'Another dare.'

'Yeh?'

'I want to get a car.'

There was a pause. 'A car?' Ash said, looking blank. 'You already did that. You did it last night. Enjoyed it, I reckon.'

I took a deep breath. 'Not just that,' I said. A foghorn wailed on the river, reminding me how lonely it was in this high-rise, with just Ash and Rainbow for company. They were both staring at me now, Rainbow confused, Ash beginning to smile his grey smile. 'I ought to twock a car,' I said, 'and then set fire to it. I ought to do that to show I respect what you do.'

There was a long silence. I could see them thinking. Rainbow's lips were moving. Ash's eyes flickered backwards and forwards across my face. They were looking for the trick, the joke, but they couldn't find it. They glanced at each other before Ash spoke.

'Why should we agree?' he asked.

'Because it's dangerous.'

'Is that why you suggested it?' he sneered.

'You think of something worse.'

Ash thought about it for a moment and then shrugged. 'She did ought to pay,' he said flatly. 'For what she said.'

'Yeh,' Rainbow agreed. 'She ought to pay.'

'Flowers ent enough respect.'

'Yeh, she ought to show respect,' Rainbow nodded, smiling at me affectionately.

'Teach her how tough it is.'

'Show her the worst.'

'Right.'

They both grinned at me then. I had them. *Yeh!*

'All right, Jo,' Ash said in a very quiet voice. 'You burn a car. That's the dare. You take a car from the Grange and burn it.'

I winced. The Grange was one of the worst estates in the town.

'43, Sullivan Way,' Ash added.

'Why there?' I asked.

'No reason,' Ash said with a grin. 'We just get to choose the place.'

'Could be anywhere,' Rainbow went on. 'Could be the end of the world. We just fancy 43, Sullivan Way, on the Grange. You can do it, Jo. Girl like you. Best twocker since Leanne.'

'You take whatever car's parked at that address,' Ash explained.

'And meet us at the Tesco car park afterwards,' Rainbow told me.

I thought about it for ten seconds. What if the car at number 43 wasn't one of the three easy ones? I might not be able to black-box anything else. I was terrified. I was shaking with fear. And I was thrilled. I would just have to take my chances. This was precisely what I was hoping for. I couldn't wait to get on with it.

'OK,' I told them. 'I'll do it.'

So there I was again, playing the game. Only this time I was on my own.

I had no trouble finding the address: Sullivan Way is the longest road on the Grange, running the length of the whole estate. Even this early in the evening, the street was deserted. A very old Astra was parked outside the house. I walked up the street and then all the way back down. I needed to steady my nerves. A dog barked savagely in one of the houses and then stopped with a yelp of fear. There were no lights on in number 43. The curtains were drawn. Silence stretched the air like a rubber band. It was a quiet street. Too quiet. I wanted televisions and music and the sound of laughter. This quiet made me sure there was a pair of eyes watching me from behind every sitting room curtain.

I walked up and down the street again. Then I kneeled down in the gutter beside the car and smashed the passenger window with the hammer Rainbow had given me. I dropped the hammer by the door. I was up and walking again immediately. I didn't want to get caught. I turned at the corner and waited. Nobody was following me. No sound. No angry voices and snarling Alsatians. I dodged down the side of a house and caught my breath, then peered round the edge of the wall: the street remained deserted. I went back, running this time, and slipped my hand through the broken window and opened the door. I was in.

I remembered everything I had been taught. It was like a film unreeling inside my mind. I had the ignition box open in seconds and wired the ignition. The Astra purred into life. He must have kept his car well maintained, whoever lived at number 43. I closed the car door and let the engine run for a few seconds, trying to control my breath.

Then I glanced up at the house.

Somebody was there. Standing at the window. I saw the curtains twitch and then I was looking straight into a man's face: unshaven, snarling with anger. I froze. The terror trickled down my spine into my hands and legs. I was immobilised. I held the steering wheel like a drowning man on a raft but I couldn't move a muscle. He could have walked out of his house and opened the car door and I wouldn't have been able to do a thing about it. I was hypnotised by blind terror.

Then the curtains were dropped and a light went on.

I slammed the car into gear and lurched forward. The engine cut. I was in the wrong gear. I glanced in panic at the window. He was not there. I leaned under the steering column and wired the Astra for the second time. Again it purred into life. The sweat was pouring down my face. My hands were slippery with sweat. The engine raced when I accidently touched the accelerator. I found first gear and glanced back at number 43. The front door was opening. I felt a genuine hair-raising terror, like hedgehogs crawling down the back of my neck. I drove off with my foot flat on the accelerator and didn't change gear until the rending of the gearbox and engine left clouds of smoke pouring out behind me.

I drove to the bottom of the endless Sullivan Way, the main highway through the estate. I was wet through with sweat. My hands kept slipping on the steering wheel and I was talking to myself. What if the man had run straight out of the house? What if he had called the police?

I was spooked. He hadn't caught me at the house and there was no sign of the police and *still* I was shaking like a frightened rabbit. Was it always like this: a mixture of terror and excitement? But this wasn't ordinary terror. This was something crawly and chilling, clambering inside my mind on dozens of flailing legs. This was worse than terror. I felt as though I could hardly breathe. My heart was pumping so quickly it hurt.

I drove straight to the Tesco car park. Rainbow was waiting at the gate, Ash was leaning against a tree. I parked the car and got out.

'Drive it to the middle of the car park,' Rainbow told me.

I got back in and drove to the middle of the car park. Ash watched me for several seconds and then stubbed out his cigarette. He walked over to the car and touched the bonnet. It was hot. He seemed pleased. He turned and studied my face. I got out of the car, not wanting to be sitting down when he was looking at me.

'You look wet,' he said gently, as if he were concerned.

'It's a hot night,' I said.

'No it isn't.'

I shrugged. 'I sweat when I'm terrified.'

Neither of them laughed.

'Did anybody see you?' Ash asked.

'Yes.'

'From the house?'

'Yes.'

'He didn't come out?'

'Not in time.'

I was shaking. A torrent of emotions rushed through my blood stream, making my body tremble and sweat: terror, apprehension, fear. My clothes were soaked. I was drenched with sheer fright. Every emotion I could imagine ever experiencing: but the main one was excitement. I had to lean against the car to prevent myself falling over.

'He didn't get hold of you?' Ash said again, a hint of relief in his flat voice.

'No.' They both sighed. Then suddenly it dawned on me. They knew. They had been there. I went cold with shock.

'You've done him before?' I said quietly.

Ash didn't speak. He was watching his brother. Rainbow avoided his eyes. But I already knew. They had set me up. They had sent me to a house they had already done.

'It was months ago,' Rainbow explained with a gruff laugh. 'He got cross. Tried to sort us out. But we knew he wouldn't catch you, Jo. You're too fast for him. Fat old git. It was just a joke. Bit of a laugh.' He sounded nervous, embarrassed.

Ash wasn't nervous.

'It was your idea, wasn't it?' he said aggressively.

'Yeh,' I said.

'Well then.'

'Right.' And if I'd been caught, I would have deserved it. The reality sent floods of ice down my back, and I pressed my face against the roof of the car, shaking. I was suddenly very tired. They went on watching me. Ash seemed indifferent, but I thought he was pleased I got back OK. He had sounded pleased. Rainbow couldn't stop grinning.

When I had control of my nerves again, I turned and looked at Rainbow. He was holding something in his hand. He reached out and waved it at me. It was a rag. I took it.

'You ever burned a car?' Ash asked.

'No.'

'Nothing to worry about.'

I took a deep breath. 'OK.' I glanced around the deserted car park. It was huge. There was nowhere to run. The single tree was the only hiding place. 'What if it blows up?' I said.

'They hardly ever blow up.'

'What if this one does?'

'We'll be blown up with it,' Rainbow said with a laugh.

I knew it was the gases inside the tank that blew up when a car exploded. An empty tank was more dangerous than a tank full of petrol. The petrol gauge on the Astra had pointed to full. But I could still feel the tears gathering behind my eyes. I brushed them away quickly. I couldn't cry now. Not after the terror of twocking the car. I couldn't show them how scared

I was. And I never let anyone see me cry. I felt my legs trembling but I forced myself to walk to the rear of the car.

They took the fuel cap off for me and stuffed the rag into the opening. It was a long rag and took a long time to drop into the tank, the end still hanging out. Rainbow handed me a box of matches. 'Light the rag, Jo,' Ash said quietly.

I broke six matches before I got one burning. 'Then we run?' I said, looking at Ash.

'Then we run.'

My hand was trembling so much I thought the flame was going to go out, but it didn't. It touched the petrol-soaked rag and flared instantly like a firework. I was running before the match went out. I was running for my life. I reached the tree and hid behind it. It wasn't a very old tree and the trunk was thin. I stared back at Rainbow and Ash. They were taking a casual walk across the car park.

'Run!' I yelled, as if I cared if they blew up with the car.

They reached the tree before the car leaped off the tarmac. White flame hit the sky. There was a roaring rush of flame. Metal began to burn and dance.

Plastic seats melted. Smoke billowed into the air.

'They never explode,' Ash said sadly.

'They just burn,' Rainbow explained.

Then they were walking away. I wanted to watch the fire. I wanted to see the flames burn against the sky.

'Come on, Jo,' Rainbow called.

'In a minute.'

'Come on.'

I followed them reluctantly. 'I was enjoying that,' I said, irritated by their indifference.

'It isn't over yet, Jo,' Ash said.

'It hasn't begun,' Rainbow grinned.

I glanced back over my shoulder and saw ghosts dancing in the flames. Far away, a police siren wailed. 'What do you mean?' I asked, but they didn't answer.

# Seventeen

We stopped for a cup of tea and a bacon buttie at an all-night tea van. The van was parked on a bit of wasteland near the fish processing factories. Shift workers visited the van during their breaks for mugs of tea and greasy bacon rolls.

'You did all right, Jo,' Rainbow told me, punching my arm and grinning with pleasure like a proud parent. 'You did good.'

'Thanks,' I muttered, still thinking about the way they'd set me up, sending me back to a house they'd already done. The thought sent a shiver down my spine, but I couldn't be too bitter: I could have ended up in a police cell, or got beaten up if the bloke had got out of his house a bit faster. I stared around the desolate wasteland, thanking my lucky stars: it was turning out to be a good evening, twocking a car and then torching it without singeing a hair. I ought to be grateful.

'You got to take risks, Jo,' Ash said, studying my face, seeing if I was all right. 'You got to experience danger in life or there isn't much point,' he added.

'I experienced danger,' I said. 'Where were you?'

They both liked that. Their laughter carried across the waste ground, and Ash offered me a cigarette to calm my nerves. 'You're a tough girl, Jo,' he smiled, striking a match.

'Yeh, sure,' I muttered. 'So what now?'

'Like we said, you did all right,' Ash said. 'But you can't just *stop*. The thing with danger is, you got to keep going on.'

I thought I'd had enough going on for one night. I'd offered to twock and torch a car, and I'd gone through with it. Now I needed a nice long rest.

But I was curious. I was reluctant to leave. They must have heard that in my voice. 'Thanks for the tea,' I said. 'I have to go.'

Rainbow held my arm. 'Listen to him, Jo,' he

said with his big beaming smile.

'The thing is,' Ash went on, 'you got to keep pushing at the limits. Try to do something new. Go beyond what anybody else has ever done. You do it once, you got to go back and do it again.'

I drank my tea, the hot liquid burning my mouth. 'No way,' I said, pulling my arm free. I still didn't run.

'Not on your own,' Ash said quickly. 'Not like the first time.'

'No way, I said.'

'To make it real,' Ash was saying. 'To make it *something.*'

There was a pause. I could hear Rainbow breathing heavily. He was excited. His eyes were shining. You wouldn't have known Ash was excited, but he seemed tense, waiting for me to answer, as if it really mattered to him what I said. I was mesmerised by their excitement.

I stood very still. 'Go back?' I asked.

'That's it.'

'To the same house?'

Rainbow snorted with amusement. 'Don't be stupid.'

'Not the same house, Jo,' Ash reassured me.

'Oh good.'

'The same street.'

'You're joking.'

'Tonight.'

'What!'

'Two more times.'

It was a ridiculous idea. It would be madness, returning to the scene of the crime. Doing it three times in the same evening would be suicide. The police would be there, after all the row I made, and if they weren't there yet, they soon would be. We would be begging to be arrested.

It was brilliant. It was dazzling. 'No way!' I said emphatically.

They laughed. They knew I didn't mean it.

And five minutes later we were walking back to the Grange. I couldn't resist it. No matter how frightened I was, I couldn't forget the excitement. I re-lived driving through the streets. I felt so tired I couldn't speak. But I was there. Ash and Rainbow walked in front and I followed, too exhausted to think of running away, even if I wanted to.

As we turned up Sullivan Way, I saw blue lights

flashing outside a house. It was number 43. A cold wind touched my face, hissing in my ear: go away, go away. Outside the house, a young man with cropped hair and tattooed arms was arguing with the police, demanding to know what they were going to do about his car. I shuddered. I was tempted to pull my anorak hood up over my head but Ash had already told me about that: keep your hood down and the police don't even see you; put it up and they are immediately suspicious. We kept walking. We walked right past the house, Ash and Rainbow laughing and telling each other jokes, me trailing sullenly behind.

Voices crackled on police radios. A blue light flashed on and off. The police never even gave us a glance.

A vein twitched at the side of my forehead, and I stumbled on the pavement, lurching into Rainbow like a drunk coming home from the pub.

'Keep walking,' Ash whispered out of the side of his mouth. I kept walking.

We saw an Escort about half a mile down the road. It was parked on the left-hand side of the road, facing away from number 43. Ash slowed down. He took his cigarettes out of his jacket pocket and stopped so that Rainbow could strike a match. I leaned against a lamppost, trying to control my breathing. Out of the corner of my eye, I could still see the blue light flashing on and off, but I couldn't hear the radio voices.

'OK,' Ash whispered, blowing smoke up to the sky and glancing up and down the street, checking the houses. 'Do it.'

Rainbow crossed the road and disappeared into the shadows at the far side of the Escort. I heard the shattering of the window, then I was following Ash to the car. Rainbow was already in the driving seat. He had the engine running before I was in the back.

'Go go go,' Ash shouted, thumping the dashboard.

'Go go go,' I yelled inside my head. I was turning to look back up the road as Rainbow slammed the Escort into first gear and we lurched forward. The engine cut.

'Argghhh,' Rainbow grunted.

Drops of sweat ran down my face.

'Do it,' Ash hissed at his brother, half turning in his seat and peering back up the road towards the police.

A car light went on. The blue lights were dancing.

Rainbow leaned under the steering column and

got the engine going again. He muttered all the time he was working. He was swearing. He crashed the Escort into first gear. We started moving forward again. Behind us, headlights were suddenly illuminating Sullivan Way like the lights in a football stadium. The headlights seemed to be moving.

'GO!' Ash screamed.

We drove to the top of Sullivan Way and turned towards the motorway. Sirens wailed furiously behind us. We were bound to get caught. I was going to spend the night in police cells after all. The sweat blinded my eyes, salty and stinging, and I couldn't see out of the rear window. Ash was yelling at Rainbow, telling him which way to go. The police sirens seemed to be coming out of the darkness from every direction.

'Head for the travellers' camp,' Ash was shouting, leaning over the seat to watch the police cars and giving his instructions at the same time.

Rainbow took a sharp left and gunned the car through the gears. The blue lights disappeared for several seconds, and then there were three of them, chasing us in convoy, their sirens going like a swarm of mosquitoes. Rainbow had his foot hard down on the accelerator. I could see the dual carriageway ahead, and the bright lights of the all-night petrol station.

We hit the roundabout at sixty and went straight across the flower beds. On the far side, our bumper crashed over the kerb and the Escort leaped into the air, landing with a shuddering crash. I felt my neck and spine jarred with the force of the landing. Ash was still leaning over the seat, trying to catch sight of the blue lights. They were not far away. Rainbow raced down a turning the other side of the roundabout and passed the petrol station. I saw a man who was filling his tank look up, his mouth wide open. The attendant in the station leaned forward to watch.

Then we were heading for the darkness beyond the petrol station, acres of wasteland and rubbish tips and the stink of the fish meal factory. Up ahead, I could see the lights of the travellers' camp. Rainbow was making straight for that.

'Why here?' I yelled at Ash.

'They're friends.'

Hitting the brakes, Rainbow took the car off the road and suddenly we were bouncing across wasteland. He cut the lights at the same moment. I had no idea where we were. The ground was uneven and full of potholes, but Rainbow seemed to know exactly where he was heading. In the pitch darkness, the blue lights of three police cars raced along the road behind us. They were making for the fish meal factory. Ash started laughing.

'Fooled,' he shouted, thumping Rainbow's shoulder.

'Give over!' Rainbow grunted, concentrating on the darkness ahead.

Then the blue lights were suddenly coming towards us. I couldn't make out how they got there. One minute they had been disappearing behind, driving towards the fish meal factory, and now they were in front of us, heading straight in our direction.

'They took the side road,' Ash said with a curse, thumping the dashboard with his fist.

'How did they know?' I gasped.

'Guessed.'

'Probably thought we were travellers,' Rainbow added.

We reached the travellers' camp minutes before the police. The sirens were wailing in the darkness, tearing the silence apart. Figures loomed out of the shadows, climbing from caravans. I saw men leaping into cars. Rainbow wound his window down and shouted to one of the men. Two of them came to the window. They seemed to know Rainbow.

'Go left,' they whispered, pointing beyond the fire.

Rainbow was pulling away as the police sirens became deafening and revolving blue lights filled the air. He spun to the left away from the fire and drove the car hard through the gears. Behind us, I could see several vehicles milling around. The travellers seemed to be setting off in all directions. As the police cars skidded to a halt, they were blocked-in by a dozen lorries and second-hand cars. There was a lot of shouting and furious blasting of car horns.

Ash and Rainbow howled with laughter.

'Chaos,' Rainbow yelled, thumping the steering wheel with both fists.

'Confusion,' Ash cried, wiping the tears from his eyes.

I could hardly speak for my excitement. I was too stunned to get the words in the right order. But the experience was beyond words anyway.

'How about that then, Jo?' Ash asked, leaning over the front seat and punching me on the knee. 'How about that?'

'Bliss,' I said dreamily, 'ecstasy,' and my delight set them off laughing all over again. But I meant it. The whole journey had been ecstasy, even the fear. It had been beyond my wildest imaginings. In fact, the fear was the best part of it.

Then I noticed Rainbow was heading back towards town.

'Where are we going now?' I asked.

The brothers glanced at each other. 'Paradise?' Ash suggested.

'Yeh, Paradise,' Rainbow agreed.

For a moment, I wasn't sure what they were talking about, then I knew they meant the amusement park on the edge of town.

Rainbow drove through town and out along the south promenade. The sea sobbed and swelled against the shores. I could see Rainbow's face in the mirror, his eyes wide with excitement. His hands trembled on the steering wheel. Tired, Ash sat motionless beside him, staring unseeing ahead. They had both come back down to earth. We drove to the far end of the promenade without speaking. We passed the Winter Gardens and drove out on the coast road towards Paradise Park.

It was locked and dark when we got there, but Rainbow drove straight through the flimsy wooden gates. I heard them splinter and break but the car hardly slowed down. Paradise was a giant theme park, an endless series of wonderful worlds. We drove straight for the Wild West. Plastic cowboys outside a saloon raised their six-shooters ready to fire, and Rainbow ploughed right through them, crunching their garish shirts and flared trousers beneath his wheels. A plastic stetson landed on the roof of the car and then rolled into the darkness. Dead cowboys littered the ground. Rainbow thumped the steering wheel. Out of the rear window, I saw a horde of screaming Sioux sitting on wooden horses, brandishing bows and arrows and feathered spears. The Sioux disappeared in the cloud of dust our wheels left behind. We were in a desert, and then suddenly the desert turned to grass and a river. We were right on the edge of the river. Then Rainbow turned the wheel and the Wild West had gone.

Ash was rocking backwards and forwards with excitement. I felt like I was inside some weird virtual reality film, and Ash and Rainbow were cartoon characters taking me for a ride. The trick would end soon. We would reach the end of the world of mirrors and plastic models and get back to the real world.

We skidded underneath the Arabian Nights' Flying Circus and I saw clouds and carpets flying over our heads, turbanned warriors threatening us with spears and rocks which never came. Rainbow was beginning to enjoy himself. He pulled a bottle of Diamond White from his jacket pocket and Ash opened the bottle. They drank together, not handing the bottle back to me. I yearned for a drink even if it did make me feel sick. If I could taste the Diamond White then I would know the dream was real. But Ash and Rainbow seemed to have forgotten me.

With a crash of gears and a yelp of delight, Rainbow bounced the Escort up onto the Mighty Dodgems Track and we veered sharply out of the way of a luridly purple Mighty Dodgem. As the rear bumpers locked, Rainbow hung on to the steering wheel and rammed the Escort into reverse. We were free. Another Mighty Dodgem loomed in front of us but we raced between two cars and hit the railings, sparks splintering the darkness.

Then we were off the track and racing towards the African Safari. I had been here with Ben. We hadn't liked it very much. Mum had refused to go with us. The Escort shot through the flimsy tent walls and immediately thick green creepers blinded the windscreen, winding themselves madly round the car. I heard the howls of wild animals and a rending animal roar tore at the air. Strange cries gurgled in the darkness. It must have been the screams of hot metal. There were more creepers lashing and flailing at the car and then a huge sickening spider battered our windscreen and bounced off with a crunching thud. Ants were suddenly crawling all over the bonnet. A giant wasp dive-bombed the passenger window on my side, repeatedly driving its head into the glass. I closed my eyes and told myself it wasn't real. I didn't believe it.

Then Rainbow was suddenly yelling, slamming down on the brakes and swerving towards a wall of man-eating flowers. 'Get out,' he shouted. 'Get out of the car.'

I opened my eyes. I thought he was talking to the spiders, but as we lurched away from the flowers, Rainbow swung the car door open and rolled free. In a mad scramble, Ash followed him. I took a quick glance at the spiders outside and shut my eyes again. No way.

'Jo!'

I opened my eyes and saw an enormous alligator coming for the car. I pushed the seat forward and I started to climb out. The Escort was still moving but slowly now, lurching and making strange noises, clanking across the writhing piles of crushed spiders. It was coming to a halt. Ash ran alongside the car and grabbed my arm and I jumped for freedom. The alligator disappeared into the shimmering undergrowth. I was free.

My feet squelched spiders and ants. I knew they were imitation. They weren't real. I knew they were only plastic, wrapped in black crinkly paper. I still screamed.

Ash and Rainbow laughed, but they were busy with their petrol-soaked rag. The Escort was stationary.

'Not again, Ash,' I pleaded, but he wasn't listening. 'You'll burn Paradise Park,' I shouted, staring round in terror at the ravenous lions and hungry panthers.

'I know,' Rainbow grinned.

They torched the Escort and we ran for the Wild West. A great roar of fire filled the air behind us. I could hear sirens and alarm bells and Sioux screaming for blood. My scalp tingled.

Then we were out on the dark road and walking away from Paradise Park. Several fire engines passed us on the road. We kept to the shadows. It seemed the right place to be. It seemed to be where we belonged.

Despite my confusion, I saw that we were walking back towards town. It was time for our third visit to Sullivan Way.

# Eighteen

Ash was totally in charge now: determined, deep into the game.

We found a white Metro and black-boxed it in seconds. The street was empty. There was no sign of life, no sound of police sirens.

'Even the police won't expect us to twock three cars in the same evening from the same street,' Ash said cheerfully as he started the Metro. 'They don't have the imagination.'

He gunned the engine and waited for me to climb into the back. Rainbow got into the passenger seat beside him. He took us back through the centre of town and out along the coast road. I thought we were going to make a return trip to Paradise Park but we drove straight past. The fire engines had dealt with the fire. Police cars were parked at the gates.

'I bet the press are there,' Ash said.

'Fame at last!' Rainbow sighed.

We drove on towards the dark of the countryside. 'I'm going to try something different,' Ash said to Rainbow after a long silence. His voice sounded odd: remote, hypnotised. I tried to see his face in the mirror as he concentrated on the road. He looked straight ahead, his eyes focused on the road, his mouth grim and determined.

'We've tried different,' Rainbow grunted. He sounded surprised. Wary. 'Three cars in one night is different.'

'Really different,' Ash said quietly.

I felt fear creeping up my back and down my spine. It met in my stomach and gave me painful cramps like food poisoning. I felt the colour drain out of my face. I was suddenly cold. I didn't want something really different to happen. With Ash and Rainbow around, trying something really different sounded extremely dangerous, if not terminal.

'I'm going to try something that will be for ever,'

Ash said in a weird monotone. 'Something nobody else has done, not since Karl Glover in 1990.'

There was a tense silence.

'Who's Karl Glover?' I asked.

Rainbow and Ash were staring at each other. 'He was our closest friend,' Ash said. I didn't like the sound of the 'was', but Ash was talking again. 'He grew up on our street,' he said. 'We did everything together. Until he went beyond the rest of us. I reckon it's time we caught him up.'

I was going to ask another question, but Rainbow interrupted. 'Nah,' he said, sounding as if he couldn't believe what Ash was suggesting, shaking his head slowly.

'Why not then?'

'Nah.'

'Rainbow!'

'We couldn't.'

'Karl did.'

'Karl was the best,' Rainbow said.

There was a brief pause, then Ash gave a tight, hard laugh. 'No, Rainbow. *We're* the best. Get it right. The best, is us.'

There was another brief pause while Rainbow

thought about this, then he sighed and grinned into the interior mirror. 'It's *us*,' he said with his happiest grin.

I wanted to ask precisely what it was that Karl Glover had done, but somehow I didn't have the courage to. I didn't really want to know. I thought I would just wait and see.

We drove slowly along the coast road. We had never driven so slowly, so carefully. The countryside was flat and uninteresting and silent, a desolate empty space only fit for sheep and cows and dandelions. The lights from a few farms shone in the distance and the far hills stood in shadows beneath the moon. It was a clear moonlit October night, and the air smelled fresh and full of autumn melancholy.

'Is it always like this?' I asked after several miles, thinking about the excitement, the terror, the bewildering roller coaster of emotions: one minute enjoying the whole thing, begging for worse and more; the next too terrified to even open my eyes.

'Like what?' Ash asked.

'*Alive*,' I said intensely.

There was a silence. Ash and Rainbow glanced at each other.

'Is it?' I repeated, as they stayed silent. But they weren't going to answer. They weren't going to make out this was all fun. If I wasn't frightened, there was no suffering for what I'd said about their grandma. There was no sacrifice.

'Forgot you were with us, Jo,' Ash said, glancing in his mirror.

'I'm with you,' I sighed. 'But I'm tired. I want to go home.'

I had dreamed about tonight, and now all I wanted to do was sleep.

I was beyond exhaustion.

'Right,' Rainbow yawned, stretching in the front of the car.

'My mum will have called the police,' I lied. She would never call the police. People on our estate don't. It's self-help when we're in trouble.

'You saw what happened in Paradise, Jo,' Ash said reasonably.

'Yes,' I agreed.

'I got to try something different, Jo,' Ash reasoned. 'I told you. You can see that. Got to try and beat the best.'

'Karl Glover?'

'That's right. You do understand.'

'What did he do?' I asked.

Ash looked shocked. 'You don't know?'

'No.'

'Ignorance,' Rainbow beamed amicably.

Ash drove with one hand, his elbow resting on the window. Cold night air filled the car. I felt drowsy. Maybe if I curled up on the back seat and went to sleep I would wake up in my own bedroom. 'Tell me, then,' I said as we continued down the road.

Ash spoke in a calm, matter-of-fact voice, as though he were announcing the football results on Saturday afternoon. 'He took a dive in one of the dykes, and jumped out before the car hit the water,' he said quietly. 'The car was a wreck. But he didn't have a bruise. He didn't even get wet.'

I woke up then. 'Let me out,' I said loudly, trying to climb over Rainbow's shoulder.

Rainbow pushed me back in my seat and turned and stared at me, as if he thought that might calm me down. 'It'll be all right, Jo. We promise.'

'It won't be all right.'

'It'll be the best.'

'There are three of us.'

'You can swim, can't you?' Rainbow said as though it was the most reasonable question in the world.

'We'll never get out,' I cried. 'Let me out.' I would have screamed, but I knew there was no point. This whole evening was my idea. Twocking cars. Having a little fun. I had no right to complain, and they wouldn't have listened anyway. I was paying my respects to their grandma. I was doing this to make up for the way I'd sneered at their life of crime. It was my way of saying sorry. And I couldn't get out of the car. I just had to sit there and wait. They were simply making sure I felt sorry.

We drove through darkness into darkness, and I didn't go to sleep. I kept my eyes open. Ash increased speed and found a deserted graveyard at the edge of a field. There was a church at the far end of the field, but no village. The village must have disappeared centuries ago. We drove through the graveyard gates and stopped.

Silence flooded round us. I had never sat in a graveyard before, and couldn't see the point now. This wasn't where we were heading. There were no dykes or rivers here, no water for a breathtaking dare. It seemed just another crazy idea, but then the whole evening had been full of crazy ideas.

Then the silence got to me and I knew why we were there. A graveyard was the only place where Ash and Rainbow could find peace in their troubled lives. The only place where nobody argued or threatened to call the police. The only place where they could be quiet. This was their escape.

After a long time, Ash started the engine. At the end of the graveyard, he turned out of the gates and headed back for the coast road. Sheep grazed in the fields, lifting their heads to watch us go by. Cows munched moodily at grass.

We drove in silence towards eternity. I knew it was coming. I could feel it shivering in the stars.

# Nineteen

Ash raced along the coast road. It was a long and winding road because the builders had to follow the course of the dykes on either side. You couldn't see them, but I knew they were there. The Metro's headlights glinted off water and weeds. The dykes were very wide and very deep. Ash drove faster and faster. He sang as he drove but I didn't know the song. I wasn't really listening. Rainbow beat out the rhythm on the dashboard. He was rocking backwards and forwards like a demented drunk. I tried to concentrate on where we were going. The road was like a horizontal death ride. There wasn't another car in sight.

'Where are we going?' I shouted, struggling to control a growing sense of panic.

'Wait and see,' Ash shouted cheerfully.

'It's a surprise,' Rainbow giggled.

I wondered if I could distract them by talking. 'Why the graveyard?' I asked, leaning over the front seat.

'We always go there,' Rainbow told me, looking surprised, as if I should have known that a graveyard was their nightly haunt.

'But why a graveyard?' I insisted.

'It brings us good luck,' Rainbow told me. 'Talking to the dead. Paying our respects.'

I shook my head. I suddenly realised that nothing would divert them from what they were about to do.

'Better climb in the front, Jo,' Rainbow was saying, leaning over and making room.

I climbed into the front seat. I was jammed between the two of them. For a moment, I wondered whether when the time came they were going to make any effort at all to escape from the car, then I saw Rainbow's hand on the door handle. He had already pulled it towards him so his door was open. I glanced to my right and saw that Ash had done the same. He was driving with one hand.

I saw the long slow bend coming. The road was swimming into darkness. I couldn't see where the bend ended. Mist was drifting across the fields from the sea. It was shrouding the roads. I thought I heard foghorns wailing to ships lost in the desolate countryside. But that wasn't possible. The road was flying towards the end of time in a fog that was as sudden as it was impenetrable.

I saw the eyes of some kind of rodent fleeing the bright headlights. I saw stars above spinning and then disappearing in the fog. Then the road lurched to the right and the cat's-eyes blinked their bewilderment. Black and white posts leaned towards us from the edge of the road, like fingers reaching for our flesh. The road had become a grass verge and we were bouncing off the black and white posts like racing cars hitting empty petrol barrels.

'Slow down,' I screamed at Ash. He put his foot down hard on the accelerator.

The last of the black and white posts broke with a sickening crack, and I clung to the front seat of the car, praying we would find the road beyond the blackness.

'Here we go, Jo,' Ash shouted, glancing to his left and grinning at me and his brother.

'Here we go, Jo,' Rainbow nodded, squeezing me gently on the arm.

Then the Metro was flying. I could smell scorched tyres. It was over.

In a blinding flash of headlights I saw my mum: a lovely eighteen year-old girl, leaning on the arm of a tall man, smiling into the camera. Then the light and the smile were gone.

# Twenty

The Metro died the death of a hero. It bounced off the black and white post and lurched to the right. Ash had let go of his door now and was fighting the steering wheel, ramming the gears down to second. The Metro skidded into another post, and splintered wood ripped along the bottom of the car. I expected a stake of wood to rip right through the car, but the sealed bottom was too strong. Then we lurched to the left and were sliding down the grassy bank towards the dyke.

'Jump!' Rainbow bellowed.

'Now!' Ash yelled.

The car headlights bounced off water. A water rat

slipped down the bank and went surging across the wide dyke. Grass and water reeds scratched at the sliding tilting car. We were being tipped over onto our side, and then the car righted itself again, lurching into the dyke. I screamed. But Ash and Rainbow weren't paying any attention to me; they were shouting at each other, struggling to open their separate doors.

Rainbow's door swung open before we hit the water, but in a moment of blind terror, I realised Ash's door had swung to and jammed.

Then we were in the dyke. With a sickening gurgling noise, the engine started to swallow water. There was a thump. I could hear the gurgling, the splutter of the dying engine, the churning froth of water. I pushed at Rainbow, trying to get him out of my way, but he was scrambling over me to get to Ash. He had seen the jammed door. Rainbow started screaming as icy cold water washed around our feet inside the car. His knee rammed into my stomach as he climbed over me and then his boots hacked at my legs. He was on top of me, pinning me down. I was crying with pain, desperate to get out from underneath him. If we didn't get out now, we would all drown.

Ash was yelling at us both to get out of the car.

He was struggling furiously with his own door, forcing his shoulder against it in a frenzy, hammering at the handle. The pressure of the water seemed to be holding the door closed. Water was lapping at the windscreen. I could see blood on Ash's hands as he fought to get free. He must have broken the window trying to force the door. When he saw what Rainbow was doing, he tried to punch him away, yelling at him to get out of the car, save himself. But Rainbow was out of control, too frenzied to simply use the other door.

I went on shouting at Rainbow but he was hysterical, almost weeping. The water was round my knees. I lunged sideways and with all my strength shoved Rainbow off me. As he fell against the gear stick he grunted with pain, but I was free. I reached out and grabbed hold of the passenger door handle. As I scrambled for a hold, the door swung open and then back into my face, and I thought I was going to be trapped. I yelled ferociously and kicked backwards, trying to find something to push against.

Then I was falling out of the car into freezing cold water. Gurgling water filled my mouth. I tried to scream but something slimy went down my throat. I gagged and flailed my arms at the grabbing weeds.

My legs were being held by something. I couldn't get out of the car. I thought it was Rainbow and then realised it was the car door, swinging back onto my legs. I kicked and kept kicking but the door wouldn't move. I couldn't breathe. I was choking. I swallowed mouthfuls of icy water and kicked again, my last desperate effort to get free, and suddenly I was out, surging up to the surface of the dyke.

My face came up covered with weed. Thick slime covered the surface of the dyke, and I found myself swallowing green scum. The car engine was still churning, sending bubbles frothing to the surface. The car was out in the middle of the dyke now, floating in deep water. I gasped for breath, and tried to clear my eyes. A water rat swam across my shoulder, trying to escape the turmoil. I hit out and went beneath the surface again, losing my balance.

When I came back to the surface I was further away from the car. It was sinking and I was swimming towards the far bank. I could hear sirens and see lights flashing along the winding road. I swam harder, desperate to get out of the freezing slime.

'Ash,' I shouted. 'Rainbow.'

My words blew bubbles in the water and I

swallowed again, choking. I had to get to the far side. I had to get to safety. Suddenly, my arms were like pistons, churning at the water. I swam. I swam so hard I could have crossed the North Sea. I was cold but I'd survived. I reached the far bank and clambered out. I cut my hands on reeds and my clothes were covered in mud. I dragged myself up the bank and collapsed, gasping for breath.

'Ash . . . Rainbow . . .' I whispered into the cold ground.

Close by, weasels shrieked in the long grass. A rabbit let out a terrifying squeal. I stared at the water behind me. Far away, blue lights and wailing sirens disturbed the night. I tried to sit up. Police cars were racing towards the dyke out of the darkness. Somebody in one of the isolated farms must have seen us speeding along the dangerous road and sounded the alarm. I felt the dark closing round me, and I tried to shout, but nobody heard, nobody was listening. I passed out.

When I came to, lights as strong as searchlights were illuminating the water. I could see beer cans and an old pram floating in the dyke. I shivered. I tried to see Ash and Rainbow but the car had almost sunk beneath the water, only the roof showing now, and there was no sign of the brothers. Then a horrible sucking noise came from the dyke, and the Metro disappeared beneath the surface, leaving a churn of dark cold water behind. In the silence, I saw policemen scrambling down the sides of the dyke, heard voices calling in the dark.

I turned and crawled away. I got into some long grass and kept crawling. When I reached a scattering of trees, I got up and started running. I stumbled across a field and fled the desolate landscape. Brilliant lights shone weirdly against the dark sky.

I ran for my life, but as I ran, I could only think of one thing: Ash and Rainbow had drowned.

# Twenty-one

Ben was awake when I got back to the tower block.
He was waiting in the corridor. My teeth were
chattering. I was cold and I couldn't stop shaking. I
knew Ash and Rainbow were dead. They couldn't
have got out of the Metro. It was like a nightmare and
I kept praying I would wake up in my bed, but of
course I wasn't asleep.

Ben was shaking my arm. 'I was worried,' he
cried, hanging on to my arm. 'I couldn't sleep.'

'Isn't Mum home?' I managed to ask through my
chattering teeth.

'You just made it. Where've you been, Jo?'

'Not now, Ben.'

I was close to crying again. I couldn't control my feelings or stop my mind on its endless round of speculation. I was still soaked from the dyke and my clothes were covered in mud and green slime. I ran a bath and dumped my clothes in the bedroom.

'I was *worried*!' Ben insisted, following me round the flat. 'I got you into this. It's all my fault.'

'No, you didn't. I got myself into it.'

'If I hadn't . . .'

'I have to get clean, Ben,' I said firmly. 'I can't look like this when Mum comes home. She'll have a fit.'

'Phew,' he said, sniffing my hair and managing a weak grin, his eyes shining with tears.

I got washed while Ben made a pot of tea. He sat on the edge of the bath while I scrubbed my hair clean. We drank the tea in silence. I didn't want to talk. Now I was safe and at home, Ben seemed all right. He relaxed. He didn't ask awkward questions. By the time Mum came home we were sitting in front of the television and I was nearly asleep.

Mum put a stop to that. 'Hello, kids,' she sighed, turning the television to the local news and collapsing onto the settee.

On the television, I saw blue lights and a big dyke. I quickly flicked the remote to another channel and an android flared from the screen, its hard eyes swivelling in search of something to eat, such as an innocent human being on the run.

'Jo!' Mum shouted, grabbing the remote and flicking back to the news.

'It is believed the car was being driven by joy riders,' a woman reporter was saying into the camera. 'The police say the vehicle, a white Metro, has been identified as a car stolen earlier this evening from Sullivan Way.'

Behind the reporter, the remains of the Metro swung in the air on the end of a chain. A crane lurched into view and steadied on the screen. The reporter ducked her head and smiled.

'A police spokesman has asked for anybody who might have seen the vehicle being stolen or driven near the scene earlier this evening to get in touch with them urgently. This is a shocking example of the kind of accident that can be caused by joy riding, and the police are most anxious to identify anybody who might have been involved in the incident. We will bring you more information on

Breakfast Morning News. This is Angie Frost saying goodnight.'

'Shocking,' Mum said, yawning and covering her mouth with her hand.

'It might be Ash and Rainbow,' Ben said.

I glanced at him quickly. He looked worried, still upset. He might tell her; he might say anything.

'Ash and Rainbow?' Mum asked, rubbing her eyes. 'Why them? They're not the only ones, love.'

'It could be anybody,' I agreed quickly. But I was beginning to panic. She only had to look into my eyes to see the truth. The minute she saw the filthy clothes in the bedroom she would know something was wrong. She would smell the dyke. 'We don't know,' I said, pretending to yawn.

'I know,' Ben interrupted.

'*How* do you know?' Mum asked, with a tired laugh. 'You mustn't upset yourself, Ben. You'll be having dreams again.'

'Everybody knows,' Ben began to say, then he saw my face and shrugged. 'Well, some people. It's just what kids are saying at school,' he grinned lamely. 'You know, fooling around. About Ash and Rainbow.'

Mum watched him for a few seconds. 'Pair of

idiots,' she said quietly, still frowning and then beginning to yawn again. 'They'll never learn.' She was relaxing now. 'It would serve them right. Anyway, shouldn't you two be in bed? It's almost one o'clock. Don't you have school tomorrow?'

We went to bed but I couldn't sleep. I lay in my bed and listened to the foghorns on the estuary. I had so many things to fill my mind, there was no hope of sleeping. In the darkness I could see Ash and Rainbow fighting in the front of the car. They must have gone under with the wreck. They must have drowned. I wondered why the police hadn't found the bodies, and then remembered the tidal waters of the dykes. The dykes all ran down to the sea, and bodies would float rapidly to the creeks and narrow channels of the coast if the tide had been on the ebb. Ash and Rainbow might be out at sea by now, or trapped among the reeds and bulrushes of the fast-flowing waters.

In the morning, Angie Frost was still awake. She looked as if she hadn't slept all night, ferreting out the news for avid news addicts. 'Good morning,' she smiled wearily into the camera. 'We have no fresh news on the tragic car accident last night at Beck Dyke, which seems to have involved joy riding.

The police have just confirmed that no bodies have been found but the chances of anybody surviving such a crash are extremely limited. The police still have no information concerning the occupants of the vehicle. They are continuing with their search.'

I couldn't eat a thing.

Mum had a bad headache from her night at the Cineplex and Ben had a snivelling cold and was complaining of fever. He didn't want to get out of bed much less go to school.

'You can't afford to be off school,' Mum said when I told her I wasn't feeling too good myself.

'I know.'

'You aren't worried about anything, are you, Jo?'

'No.'

'You would tell me?'

I gave her a smile and a big hug. 'I'm not worried about a thing,' I said. 'I just don't feel like going to school.'

'OK,' she smiled. 'You do look tired. I'll ring for you.'

She went through to the hall to make the call. While she did that, I grabbed a black bag and ran to the bedroom. I stuffed the clothes into the bag and hid it underneath the bed. I was back in the kitchen before she finished the call. I could take the clothes to the laundrette when she went to work.

'They know you aren't going in,' she said, and went to sit in the bathroom where she could have a cigarette in peace. I sat in the kitchen, drinking tea and trembling.

At eleven in the morning, we all sat in front of the television with cups of black coffee while Angie Frost told us that the police were still looking for bodies and that the coastguards were watching the main outlet from the dyke into the tidal basin. Nothing had been found. 'The search will not be abandoned until the bodies are recovered,' Angie told us with an exhausted smile, the black bags under her eyes swollen and yellowing like bruises, her lipstick garish in the morning light.

'Oh no,' Mum said.

Angie carried on. 'The vehicle is at the police wrecked-vehicles pound,' she explained. 'A 1989 Metro, stolen from Sullivan Way early yesterday evening. The police would be grateful for any witnesses who may have been in the vicinity to come forward.'

I was beginning to wish I'd gone to school.

I offered to go in to town to collect the local newspaper, and when I reached town, went into McDonald's and blew a week's money on cheeseburgers and french fries. I needed the energy. I wanted something to make my mind come alive, pierce the overwhelming tiredness that seemed to have descended ever since last night. I sat at the window and gorged, praying for help.

Then I saw Leanne walking down the street. I watched her. She was getting nearer. She was walking straight past the window where I was sitting. There were tears pouring down her face. I doubted if she knew where she was going.

I lifted my hand to attract her attention, but she didn't see me. I left the remains of my food and rushed out into the street but she was gone. I ran to the end of the street. A man elbowed me off the pavement and I swore and dodged out of his way, a car braking hard and swerving as I ran into the road. At the corner, I looked round for Leanne but there was no sign of her.

I started to walk back to the estate. I walked slowly, in a daze. I kept thinking about Ash, his grey clothes and cold eyes. I kept thinking about Rainbow's smile, the way he held me that first night in the high-rise. I couldn't bear to think of him in the car in the cold dyke. I wanted to say his name, but my mouth wouldn't say the word. I don't know how long I was walking before I got home. When I reached the tower block, somebody was waiting for me in the shadows of the main entrance.

It was Leanne.

'Leanne?'

'I had to come and see you, Jo.' She was still crying. I felt my own eyes fill with tears.

'Don't cry, Leanne, please.' I wanted to put my arm round her shoulders. I wanted to comfort her, say something to stop the tears. She was desperate. The bags beneath her eyes were yellowing with tiredness.

'Have you seen Ash? Do you know what happened?'

'Leanne . . .'

'I know you went with them. I know you were there.'

I couldn't tell her. I couldn't say I was there. I suddenly felt guilty just for being there, but I didn't stop them getting out of the car, if they died it was because Rainbow wouldn't leave Ash, he wouldn't leave him . . .

'Leanne, you mustn't be upset.'

'I can't help crying. I know something's happened to Ash. I know he's gone. I love him. I love him. Nobody knows. Tell me what happened, Jo, please.'

She was sobbing. Her mascara ran down her cheeks. Her eyes were red. She pushed her black hair back out of her eyes and bit back the tears, helpless with grief and bewilderment.

I tried to comfort her, but I had nothing to say. I couldn't admit to being in the car. I couldn't say the words. Because I knew the words would make me cry and I didn't want to cry in front of Leanne.

'I don't know what happened,' I said brusquely, my throat aching as I forced the words out.

'Weren't you there?' she asked.

'No,' I lied.

'Didn't you go?'

'I was frightened,' I said, letting the words lie for me. I knew she would believe me. I knew they all thought I was straight and told the truth. I lied, and it was easy to trick her. She dried her eyes and walked away, but I felt a lump in my throat as I watched her hunched shoulders, the hopelessness in her eyes. She never looked back. I felt as though my heart were breaking.

I stood outside the tower block for a long time. I had forgotten all about buying a newspaper. It didn't seem important.

# Twenty-two

I had a temperature by the evening and a painful headache. I was feverish, hot one minute and shivering the next. Sweat ran down my face and the back of my neck. Mum put me to bed and told Ben to give me plenty of drinks. She had to go to the Cineplex. We couldn't survive without the extra money and they would sack her if she went off ill. You had to die before the Cineplex would let you stay at home.

Ben was watching television. I closed my eyes and listened to the shrieks of the audience: some deep intellectual game show where the host poured gunge over the guests and blonde bimbos simpered and bounced for the cameras. When I was healthy I liked that kind of stuff, but now that I was ill the noise travelling through the bedroom walls got on my nerves. I wanted silence. I wanted endless peace and tranquility away from Noel Edmonds.

I must have drifted into sleep. When I opened my eyes, Ash and Rainbow were sitting beside my bed. Ben was standing by the door.

I scrambled back against the wall. I was shocked, scared. They were real. I reached out and touched Ash's arm. I wanted to shout for joy.

'How did you get in here?' I asked, laughing with relief and fright. I was glad to see them, and yet I never wanted to see them again.

'Ben opened the door,' Ash said quietly. 'How else would we get in?'

I glanced quickly at Ben, hovering by the door. I didn't really want him here in the room, not with Ash and Rainbow. I didn't want him to hear our conversation. 'I thought you were watching television?' I said.

He looked doubtful, worried. He kept glancing at Ash and Rainbow as if he expected them to attack me. 'Is it all right?' he asked.

'Fine,' I nodded.

'OK.' He wandered off, going back to watch the television.

Ash closed the door quietly. He smiled at me complacently. He was wearing a new grey sweatshirt and black jeans and a pair of black and grey trainers. He looked even more mournful than usual. Rainbow was as colourful as ever, with his orange and green Mohican stripe and a shining black eye. He must have caught his face on the Metro's door as they scrambled to safety. I still couldn't believe they'd managed to get free. Rainbow was wearing fresh clothes as well, and a pair of red DMs.

'I thought you were dead,' I said in a whisper. 'How did you get out of the car? How did you get away?'

'Same as you,' Rainbow said as if I was really thick.

'Ash's door was jammed,' I said. 'I didn't see you get out. I thought you must've been trapped.'

'Forced the door, didn't we,' Rainbow said. He laughed. 'You think we're just going to drown, Jo?'

I shook my head, laughing, tears in my eyes. 'I thought you were drowned,' I kept repeating, as though they were the only words I could say.

'No way.'

'Have you been home?' I asked.

'Daren't risk it,' Ash said. 'Been hiding in a barn. Slept there all day until it was safe. We often sleep out, Jo. Doing the town. You can always find somewhere to sleep if you're tired enough.'

'Then where did you get the new clothes?' I asked.

'Visited a shop we know. You can always find gear to wear, Jo.'

So they must have come straight here. I closed my eyes and felt sweat running down my face. I suddenly felt ill again. I understood now why Leanne was so sarcastic about twocking. It ended up like this, with misery and trouble and the terror of friends maybe being dead, and you not knowing, for hours and hours.

I thought about Leanne again, suddenly realising she didn't know they were still alive. I sat up. 'Have you seen Leanne?'

Ash shook his head. 'We're going round her place now.'

'She's worried,' I said angrily. 'Don't you realise?'

'It's OK, Jo,' Rainbow said. 'We're going round there. We had to see you first.'

'Don't you *care* how much you hurt people?' I said furiously. 'She *loves* you, Ash!'

Ash stood up, then sat down just as quickly, controlling his temper. 'The quicker we get out of here the quicker she'll know, then,' he said reasonably, smiling at me. 'We just wanted to tell you something.'

'I don't want to know,' I said tiredly. 'Just go.'

There was a long pause. Ash waited for me to look up.

I couldn't believe he didn't want to go straight round to Leanne's and reassure her.

'It didn't work, Jo,' Ash said quietly.

'What didn't work?'

Rainbow sighed with impatience. Ash looked irritated. 'You know I said I was going to try something different,' he said carefully, as if he was explaining something to a child, 'to beat the records? To beat what Karl Glover did, once and for all?'

'Yeh,' I nodded impatiently.

'It didn't work. It didn't make me feel better. It didn't take me beyond where I'd already been.'

'So?' I said, glaring at Ash.

There was another long silence. The silence had a cold clammy dankness about it which reminded me of the dyke and made me shiver.

'It isn't over, Jo,' Ash said after a pause.

'What isn't over?' I asked. But I knew what Ash was going to say. I knew they wanted to go twocking again. I knew they wanted me to go with them.

And I couldn't turn away. I couldn't refuse to listen. I was trapped in their ridiculous nightmare. I was trapped by the speed and the dares, and by something else, something really frightening: after everything that had happened, I couldn't live without the excitement I still felt whenever I was near Ash and Rainbow. I couldn't imagine life without the terror they brought with them: I didn't want to imagine it.

Nobody spoke.

Rainbow looked uncomfortable. He kept glancing at his brother, rubbing his nose with the back of his hand. He smiled at me, as if we were talking about the weather.

I didn't even pretend to argue. 'What do you want me to do?' I asked Ash flatly, my voice sounding as if it came from a long way away.

'Another dare,' Ash said simply.

'Yeh.'

'To end it, you know,' he said, raising his

eyebrows, making sure I got the point.

'Yeh.'

'You meet us tomorrow night.'

'Where?'

'In the graveyard.'

'You must be joking,' I laughed, my mouth dry with nerves.

'Safest place,' Ash said reasonably. 'Nobody knows about it except us three and Leanne. Safest place on earth.'

'Yeh. Is that all?'

'No.'

'Don't tell me.'

'You got to bring a car.'

'*You* bring the car,' I said angrily.

'We're going to,' Rainbow said. 'We're going to bring a Metro. Make sure you bring the same, Jo. A new Metro.'

I stared at them in disbelief. 'Any particular colour?' I asked, but the sneer never reached my voice. They weren't listening anyway.

'A new Metro,' Ash nodded. 'The latest you can find.'

'Right,' I said impatiently. Now that it was agreed,

I wanted them out of the flat. I didn't want them to be here when Mum got home.

'So you bring the car,' Ash said. 'Right?'

'Right.'

'And we'll see who can dare.'

I'd had enough. 'Are you going to see Leanne now?' I asked angrily.

'Course we are,' Rainbow nodded. 'We'll see Leanne then get some sleep. See you tomorrow night. You take care, Jo.'

Then they were gone as abruptly as they had arrived.

# Twenty-three

Leanne came round the following afternoon.

I was still feverish, my temperature in the high nineties, my head aching like a huge bruise. I was sitting at the window, staring down to the docks and the estuary, when I heard the knocking on the door.

She was smiling. 'You lied, Jo. You were there.'

So she had seen Ash and Rainbow. Did she know they'd been here? 'I didn't know they were alive,' I said defensively, my face flushing hot and my eyes watering. 'I couldn't tell you, Leanne. I didn't know what to say . . .'

She touched my arm. 'It's OK, really. Can I come in?'

'If you like.'

'How about a coffee?'

I nodded towards the kitchen and she went and put the kettle on. It seemed funny, seeing her in the flat, like we were mates, close friends: the thing I had dreamed about a few days ago. I sat down at the window and went on staring out to the estuary. I seemed to have lost the ability to speak. Leanne made the coffee and came and sat with me. She had put plenty of sugar into the cups. I drank the sweet hot coffee and felt better. My eyes filled with tears again: gratitude and exhaustion. She didn't hate me. It was all right.

'Did Ash and Rainbow send you?'

'No.'

'No?' I said with surprise.

'They don't know I'm here.'

'I see,' I said thoughtfully, not seeing at all. 'Then why are you here?'

'They said you were going to take another dare,' she said simply. It wasn't a question.

'Ahh,' I said, trying to look as if I'd just remembered.

'To end it,' she said ironically.

I didn't respond for a while until eventually I said, 'That's right.'

There was a long silence. I couldn't think of anything to say. I was wondering why she'd come round, and now she seemed to have gone a long way away. She was thinking, staring out of the window. I watched her, not wanting to disturb her thoughts. She was beautiful, with her white face and black hair. Suddenly, she shook her head and glanced up at me. Her eyes were a very pale blue.

'I think we have to talk,' she said kindly.

'Why?' I said.

'Because I want to. Because I went twocking for years and I know what it's like. I know how you feel. Because it nearly got you killed last night and I don't want to lose you.'

I was touched by her concern and my eyes filled with tears. 'What about Ash and Rainbow?' I muttered.

She shook her head briefly. 'I can't do anything about Ash,' she said. 'Or Rainbow.' She didn't want to talk about them, or couldn't bear to.

I stared at her in silence. I was having difficulty sorting all the thoughts in my head. I didn't want to talk about joy riding. I wanted to go and do it, and I didn't see how Leanne could help me get over *that*. And she couldn't control Ash and Rainbow any more than I could. They would do what they wanted.

'I don't see the point in talking,' I said sullenly.

Leanne turned and stared out of the window again. Lost in her own thoughts, she lit a cigarette and smoked quietly. There was a long silence.

'You don't have to go,' she said eventually.

'So?' When I looked up again, I saw the smile on her face. 'What's funny?'

'You are.'

'Thanks.'

She lit another cigarette and offered me the packet. 'You want to go,' she said when I had a cigarette lit.

'Maybe.'

'No, not maybe, you *want* to go, at least be honest.'

'OK,' I said with a scowl, making Leanne laugh out loud.

'Say it!'

'OK!'

'It's hard work, talking to some people,' she said with a tight laugh.

'I said OK, didn't I?'

She wasn't listening. She was lost in her own thoughts again.

'I suppose you can change the future by interfering,' she said with a vague smile.

'I don't have much of a future at the moment,' I said bleakly.

She turned from the window and looked at me. I noticed her eyes were alive, full of kindness and sympathy, as if she understood exactly what kind of whirlwind I was going through: addicted to the excitement; longing for the speed and the danger.

She rubbed the side of her face. She looked preoccupied, almost grieving. 'You must never say that,' she said softly.

'It's true.'

'You must never say it,' she said again, her voice harsh and grating.

We stared at each other for a long time.

I shrugged. 'OK.'

'OK,' she said with a smile. She turned back to the window and the estuary. 'I don't think people should take dares,' she said. 'Dares are for people who're frightened to be themselves.'

I knew then she was talking about herself. I

thought she was going to tell me the one thing I didn't want to hear: forget it, don't take the dare, it's death row with a vengeance. I thought she was going to say the very words that were nagging at the back of my mind: stay at home and forget it, this is something you don't need to do, this is stupid and dangerous and not your business.

And I felt dreadful: disappointed, depressed, miserable. I wanted to go back to Ash and Rainbow and meet them in their graveyard. I wanted the nightmare adventure to go on, like a game where you can't get off the roller coaster. I never wanted it to end.

But Leanne didn't say these things. She *knew*. She stared straight out of the window into the autumn sunlight.

'Dares are for stupid people,' she went on quietly. 'They're for the second-rate.' She paused dramatically, staring right into my eyes as though she was trying to get inside my mind. I felt like she was searching my soul.

'Yes?' I prompted her impatiently.

'Sometimes we can't not go,' she said.

I didn't know what she was talking about, but

suddenly it was thrilling, disturbing. It made my heart beat faster. I watched her, hypnotised by her words, her calm voice.

'Then I should go!' I said excitedly. 'I should do it!'

'No, Jo,' she said urgently. 'I didn't say that.'

'I don't understand . . . You said . . .'

'You have to make your own decision,' she almost shouted. 'You have to make your own choice.'

I stared at her, confused, miserable. I felt lost. I took a mouthful of smoke and swallowed hard. 'Why don't you just say "Don't go"?' I asked sullenly. 'That's what you really think.'

She was still looking at me, watchful, hard. She turned away. 'Because I always went when it was me,' she said quietly. 'Because I know how much you want to go.'

A gloom settled on the room then. I heard a siren wailing out at the estuary. Gulls cried mournfully along the shores. There was no sound from the deserted streets below. In the silence, all I could hear was the sound of my own desires: I wanted to take the dare.

'I'll go,' I said after a long pause.

'That's up to you, Jo.'

'I *want* to go.'

'I know.' She stumbled over the words, and turned away, hiding her tears.

'Leanne?'

'I'm OK.'

She wasn't, but I daren't reach out and touch her. She was somewhere very private. She forced a smile and shrugged, blowing her nose on a tissue and drying her eyes. I knew it was Ash she was upset about, not me.

'Why don't you tell Ash to *stop*?' I asked angrily, upset by her distress.

She shook her head wearily. 'He won't stop.'

'If you told him . . .'

'He's destroying himself, Jo, he goes on and on and on, he won't stop until it's all over.'

'You stopped,' I said.

'Yeh.'

'So!'

She shrugged. 'I did some dreadful things. Fearful. And it was getting worse. I kept telling myself I could stop whenever I wanted, then one night I realised I didn't *want* to stop. That's when I knew it was out of control. So I just said "Sod it" and carried on. Then I got bored. I get bored, Jo. I'm lucky that way. I wanted to do other things. So I just stopped, like giving up smoking.'

'You haven't given up smoking,' I said.

'No,' she smiled, then looked straight at me. 'But when I want to, I just will. That's how it is.'

'You came the other night,' I pointed out unkindly. 'You were having a good time then.'

Leanne didn't speak.

I stared out of the window, thinking about Ash. If you loved somebody, wouldn't you do anything they wanted? Rainbow's crazy smile flickered across my mind. 'I think Ash is selfish,' I said, resenting the confused feelings, wanting the night to come when things would be so much simpler.

'Not like you?' Leanne smiled quietly.

'It's new for me. It's what I want. They've always been selfish, Ash and Rainbow, the things they've done.'

'You didn't know them when they were young,' she said.

'I did,' I told her. 'We went to the same school.'

'You never really knew them, Jo. Not when they

were little. Before their mum went away and their dad died.' Her voice was tight, choking. I saw the pain in her eyes.

I thought the darkness had come right inside me then: the unhappiness of Ash and Rainbow's lives. I heard Leanne's words but they seemed to travel from a long way away. My head was reeling.

'It was when their dad died they changed. I don't know why Ash called himself Ash. He once got burned by a firework, but he laughs about that. Rainbow always liked rainbows. When he was a little boy he said he wanted to be a painter. He stopped painting when his mother left home. She went away with a man she loved. Their dad should have stayed and looked after them, but he couldn't stand the loneliness. It was a dreadful thing to do, but people do dreadful things sometimes. They changed after he was gone. They stopped laughing. All the laughter went out of their eyes.'

I couldn't think of anything to say.

After a long silence, she looked up at me and smiled. It was a weary smile, tired. 'You understand?'

'Yes.'

She nodded to herself and got up to leave.

I took a deep breath. 'I am going to go,' I said. 'This dare. I am going to do it.'

She didn't say anything for a moment. She stood up and put her cigarettes and lighter back into her bag. 'Take care,' she said. She walked quickly to the door and opened it.

'Leanne!' I wanted to follow her, stop her. I wanted her to say it was all right.

She turned and stared at me. 'I know you have to do it, Jo,' she said. 'I was just the same.'

Then she was gone.

# Twenty-four

I sat alone for the rest of the afternoon, thinking about the things Leanne had said.

She was right about Ash's dare. The minute she left the room, I knew nothing had changed. If Ash and Rainbow dared me to ride off the end of the Pier, I wouldn't be able to resist. It was like a drug. It was a drug. And worse than cigarettes. I could always say no to cigarettes. This was something really dangerous, and I couldn't imagine saying no.

I kneeled down beside the chair where Leanne had been sitting, and I cried. I was frightened. I didn't know how I was going to get myself out of the situation I had found myself in, but deep inside I knew

I didn't want to get out of it. For the whole afternoon, I struggled to see clearly, and all I could see was that I had already made my choice: I wanted to accept the dare.

And then it was time to go. One more time.

I left the flat in the evening and walked to the Grange. I had a long way to go if I was going to keep my appointment with Ash and Rainbow in the graveyard. I wasn't even sure I could find it again. I found a Metro in one of the first roads on the estate and broke the passenger window with a stone I'd picked up from the gutter. I opened the door, kneeled down and started the engine. It went like a dream. The ignition worked first time. I gripped the steering wheel and felt the sweat running down my hands. I found first gear and started down the long deserted road back to the graveyard.

It was cold and foggy. A thin mist drifted off the sea and foghorns moaned like prehistoric animals at the estuary. The streets of town were deserted, and a thin drizzle fell through the fog, blowing against the windscreen. It was the sort of night when you want to get on the motorway and drive forever. I drove slowly, the car window down, enjoying the sense of freedom you get in a car, the feeling that you can just drive off anywhere and leave your old life behind, provided you have enough petrol.

I drove past the Cineplex, and saw my mum walking head down in the rain, hurrying for work. She didn't notice me in the car. She looked sad and alone, and my heart ached for her, working at a job she hated just to bring in extra money, trying to manage without my dad. He would have been proud of her, if he cared. Anybody would.

Then I was out of town, taking the same coast road Ash had taken. There were no lights out here. The rain got heavier. The engine purred happily. It was a good car. I wouldn't have worked so smoothly if I'd been a car and somebody had smashed one of my windows and black-boxed me to get me going. I would have refused to start, or cut out at important moments. In a strange mood, I squeezed the steering wheel and felt real affection for the vehicle that was taking me to the graveyard.

Ash and Rainbow were waiting for me behind the tombstones. Ash was leaning against a Victorian angel, and Rainbow was sitting on a family tomb, listening to his Walkman. Their Metro was parked a few yards away. I drove up the narrow track that ran through the heart of the graveyard, and when I saw them, cut the engine. The silence flooded in from the fields.

'You took your time,' Ash said, still leaning against the angel. In the rain, the angel looked as if she was crying. 'I thought you'd decided not to take the dare,' Ash said with his harsh smile.

I got out of the car and shrugged. I glanced round. In a corner of my mind, I saw Leanne walking towards me, and I felt strangely comforted, as though she knew what was going on. I swallowed hard, and Leanne wasn't there any more.

Ash stared at me for a long time. I didn't drop my eyes. He had this frightening gift for appearing to be able to read your mind. I knew he was reading mine. He concentrated hard and I could feel his intensity going inside my head. I looked away but it was no good.

'Leanne came to see you?' he said quietly.

I nodded, surprised.

'This afternoon?'

'Yes.'

He thought for a moment. 'Did she try and change your mind?'

'Yes.'

There was another brief pause.

'That's fine.'

'Is it?' I asked. 'I don't get it, Ash. I don't get any of it. You don't need to prove anything. You've already proved how tough you are driving into the dyke. Nobody thinks you're scared. Are you trying to frighten me? You don't need to try, you already frighten me.'

'Then why are you here?' he shouted.

'Because I like it,' I yelled.

There was a long silence. Ash watched me, surprised by my outburst, then with a sudden angry movement, he walked away from the weeping angel. He tapped his brother on the shoulder and Rainbow jumped, as if woken from a deep sleep. He ripped the Walkman away from his ears.

'Wot?' he asked, staring sharply at his brother.

Ash touched his shoulder again, pausing to look at him. They stared into each other's eyes.

'It's time, Rainbow.'

'Yeh?' Rainbow grunted.

'Yeh.'

Then Ash walked to their car and climbed into the

driving seat. Rainbow got into the passenger seat beside him. I got back into my own Metro. I touched the steering wheel and felt comfortable, saying hello to an old friend. I closed the door and wound the window down. All around me angels and tombstones stood in dark shadows. The fog was getting denser, and I could hear foghorns not far away. We were close to the sea.

'Where to?' I called, starting the engine.

'The promenade,' Ash said.

'The promenade,' Rainbow echoed.

My stomach lurched. My pulse leaped, a sudden dizzying sickness. The promenade and the sea wall. A ten-foot drop into the sea. I should have known.

In his own excitement, Rainbow punched the air. 'Yeh!'

# Twenty-five

We drove to the promenade, Ash and Rainbow leading the way. They stopped at the Pier. I pulled up alongside them seconds later. I got out of the car and breathed the night air. The fog was beginning to drift and clear. The promenade was deserted, two miles of darkness disappearing into the sea. The sea suddenly seemed very close, the high tide lapping against the sands and the metal struts of the old pier. It was a Victorian pier, old as the seaside resort and derelict now that nobody visited piers anymore.

'Here we are,' Ash said, getting out of the other car.

Rainbow followed him. 'Here we are, Jo,' he said

with his barking laugh, punching me affectionately on the shoulder.

I leaned against the door of my Metro. I could smell the sea, filling the car, filling my lungs. We were swimming into a sea of darkness and cold, something ancient and not kind, something wicked and full of malice. There would be no escape tonight.

'What do you want me to do?' I asked.

'The dare,' Ash said quietly, his voice tense with excitement.

'The *last* dare, Ash,' his brother reminded him.

'That's right, Rainbow. The *last* dare. Nobody will top this.'

'You haven't tried it before?' I asked. 'Whatever it is.'

'No, we haven't tried it before, Jo,' Ash agreed.

'And do you think it will work? Will it be enough to satisfy you? To stop you?'

'Maybe,' Ash said, deliberately winding me up.

'I hope so,' Rainbow sighed. For the first time, I had a hint that Rainbow had had enough.

I had one last question. 'Why me?'

Ash laughed briefly. 'Oh, it had to be you, Jo.'

'Why?'

'Because we like you,' Ash said simply.

'Yeh,' Rainbow nodded. 'Because we like you.'

I closed my eyes and said a quick prayer. It was going to take more than prayer, but tonight seemed a good night to start praying. I opened my eyes when I was ready and took a last smile at the rapidly thinning fog. I had grown up round here. I had played wild games on this pier. I wasn't ready to go, but it was now or never.

'OK, what is it, then?' I asked.

'The dare?' Ash queried.

'Yes. The dare.'

Ash thought for a second and then laughed. 'You have to drive to the end of the promenade at top speed,' he said. 'You have to race us to the end of the promenade.'

'Then?'

'Then?' Ash said with an incredulous laugh.

'Yes, *then*,' I insisted.

'Then you brake, Jo. Even you could work that one out. You brake. First one to brake is the loser. Last one to brake wins the dare.'

I laughed.

The promenade ended at the sea wall and then

there was a drop of ten feet down to the sea. Not much more than the slide into the dyke, if our brakes just happened to fail. Then we went over the wall. And it was high tide tonight. If the fall didn't kill us, the sea would.

How could I resist such a challenge!

'I'm not doing it,' I said weakly, one last pathetic gesture towards reality.

Ash obviously didn't believe me. He mocked me with his cold eyes. 'Why not?' he asked sarcastically.

'If our brakes fail we'll drown?' I suggested.

'You did it before,' Ash pointed out. 'At the dyke.'

'I didn't have much choice then.'

'Just go over the wall and fly,' Rainbow said with a bright laugh.

I wondered if he was drunk.

'Don't you understand, Jo?' Ash asked seriously. 'All you have to do is brake. You'll be the one driving the car this time. You can brake whenever you want. You just lose the dare.'

I took a deep breath. There didn't seem to be much room for escape. If I tried to walk away now they would probably take me in their own vehicle. I wouldn't put it past them. At least if I drove myself I could stop – if I wanted.

I knew I was going to go. There are some dares you have to take, some challenges you can't turn down. I felt a thrill of danger as I heard the words in my mind.

'So,' I said after a moment, more to myself than them.

'You going to do it?' Rainbow asked. I could see him watching me curiously, wanting to find out how far I would go, whether I was one of them.

I nodded.

He turned and said something to Ash I couldn't hear. They both looked at me. To my surprise, Rainbow seemed confused, uncertain.

'What is it?' I asked.

He shrugged, rubbing his fist across his broken nose. For a moment, he looked like Ben, struggling to find words. Then he gave up.

'You're OK, Jo.'

'You too, Rainbow.'

He nodded, hesitating, and then reached out clumsily and touched my arm. Just a light touch. A stroke. A sign of affection. He smiled, then walked away. I hadn't imagined he could be so gentle.

I climbed into the Metro and put the car into gear and gunned the engine. Ash and Rainbow did the same. I put the gear into neutral and stared straight ahead. I was ready.

I glanced across to the other car. They were both smiling. They were more than ready to go.

'When do we start?' I shouted through the open window.

'When I say the word,' Ash yelled.

'What word?'

Ash and Rainbow glanced at each other, then Rainbow leaned out of his window. 'Speedwell,' he shouted.

'Are you going to tell me what it means?' I said.

Ash leaned forward and watched me. He thought for a moment, deciding, weighing things up, then nodded briefly to his brother.

'It's a cave we went down one summer,' Rainbow said.

'A cave?'

'In Derbyshire. On a holiday.' I knew he meant when they had a father. A holiday with their father, a long time ago. I could understand that.

I might have said something similar about my own father, except he never took me down any caves. But he took me to funfairs and circuses. He played football with me on the grass behind the tower block.

I revved the engine again and felt the car throb with power and life, responding to my delicate touch on the accelerator. I gripped the steering wheel.

It was time to go.

# Twenty-six

We were off.

I found second gear as the other Metro bounced off the first of the retarders. When I hit the retarder, my car lurched to the left, and I righted it, spinning the steering wheel into the skid to try to keep control. Ash was already in third gear, beginning to pull ahead. I could see Rainbow jumping up and down in the seat beside him.

'No you don't,' I shouted, thumping the steering wheel and crashing my own Metro up into third gear as I sped towards the second retarder.

I was already in the race. I was already determined to win. I had all but forgotten what waited for the winner at the end of the road.

As the Metro thumped off the second retarder, I thought my stomach was going to go through the floor of the car, the force of the impact jarring my elbow against the door handle. I lost the wheel. The Metro lurched to the right this time, skidding wildly towards the sea.

Ash was already yards ahead. Gritting my teeth, I changed gear and clung to the steering wheel.

In third gear, the speedometer touched forty-five and I collided with the kerb, the car juddering at the rending crash and then metal screaming angrily as I scraped along the edge of the pavement. I spun the wheel again and swerved back across the road to the other side of the promenade. I was sweating and my head ached. My elbow was numb from the jarring blow against the door handle. This was worse than the dodgems and I was doing all the damage myself with my carelessness. I had to concentrate. I had to keep control of the car.

I let the steering wheel spin into the skid and took my foot off the accelerator. The tyres threw clouds of spray up from the wet road. I hit the far kerb with another shuddering impact, the hubcaps screeching and grinding along the edge of the pavement, a shower of sparks splintering the darkness. The sparks scattered behind me like fireworks, as at last I got the car into the middle of the road, putting my foot back down on the accelerator, racing after Ash and Rainbow along the deserted promenade.

I had reached fourth gear by the time we reached the railway station. The lights of the Pier had already faded behind me, and along the tideline I could see white surf in the headlights of the car. The slow curving bend of the estuary was already bringing the sea closer and closer to the promenade. A man was walking a dog along the foreshore, and he stopped and watched as our two cars raced through the night.

I pressed my foot down hard on the accelerator and drew level with the other Metro as we passed the clock tower on the railway station. The railway tracks ran the length of the promenade, behind the amusement arcades and gift shops. I could see Rainbow jumping up and down inside his car, yelling and beating the side of the door with his fist. I had my window down and I could hear him. 'Go go go,' he was shouting, glancing at me, yelling at Ash.

'Go go go,' I yelled back.

I saw the big dipper and the big wheel on my right, silent against the night sky, towering above the white sands. The big wheel seemed to be spinning as we raced past. I thought I heard ghostly fairground music jangling in the drizzle of rain. Then the big wheel was gone, and there were roundabouts and golden gallopers, swingboats and a helter-skelter. A mini-dodgem ride stood empty without its cars. All the rides were sheeted down for the winter. The beaches were deserted.

'Go go go,' I yelled into the darkness.

The Metro responded to my lightest touch, the headlights illuminating the cafés and amusement arcades on my left, the fairground rides down on the beach. Beyond the rides there was the darkness of the sea pounding up the shores. Fifty miles an hour seemed like five hundred as I hit another retarder and the tyres banged and burned the air, a thumping ride that jarred every nerve in my body.

'Go go go,' Rainbow was shrieking in the other car, waving his fist at me in his excitement. Ash was staring fixedly ahead.

I concentrated all my being into the steering wheel. I had visions of skidding on the wet retarders and hitting the metal railings along the railway track behind the arcades. I had visions of being catapulted high into the air on the other side of the promenade and dropping down to the sea in a series of stomach-churning somersaults, burning metal sinking beneath the surface of the sea. I wanted to be in complete control when I had to brake.

The seconds went by as slowly as centuries. I lived every moment. I was alive with terror and concentration. My face was soaked with sweat and my hands ached from gripping the steering wheel. My back was rigid with tension. The car was doing seventy miles an hour now and Ash and Rainbow were still right there alongside me. My body had become part of the Metro, my only friend on this weird journey.

Then we were past the rows of candyfloss stalls and arcades and Wonderland loomed out of the darkness at the end of the promenade. Beyond Wonderland there was only the sea. I began to edge ahead of Ash and Rainbow, and thought they were slowing down, but it was my Metro gaining speed. I saw the pear-shaped domes of Wonderland to my left, and lights of ships far out at the estuary to my right.

Ash and Rainbow were level again, and I could see Ash forcing himself back in his seat, slamming his foot down on the accelerator. Imperceptibly, Ash and Rainbow regained the lead.

I flinched, almost losing the steering wheel as a white bird shot past my windscreen. Then the bird was gone and there was only the darkness ahead.

And the railings. In the headlights of the two cars, the railings at the far end of the promenade raced towards us. I could see waves breaking over the sea wall, spray boiling in the darkness. I heard Rainbow give a yell of excitement. Ash blasted his car horn.

At seventy miles an hour we were racing straight for the metal railings at the end of the promenade. Beyond the railings was the sea wall, and a drop of ten feet into the dark merciless waters of the sea.

Nobody could survive that drop.

I looked into the mirror. There was nobody behind us: no blue lights flashing a message of salvation, no fire engines clamouring to set us free, no ambulances racing to save our lives.

I looked back towards the railings ahead and guessed I had seconds to live. Ash was not going to stop. He was going to go over the sea wall and drown.

There would be no happy ending for Ash and Rainbow, only a plunging journey down into a watery death.

I took a final look into the other car. I blinked, losing concentration for a split-second and two strange faces greeted me in the darkness.

Rainbow had lost all his colour. His face was white. His head looked round and pale. He looked like an albino. He was a frightened teenager, his chin wobbling with terror, his eyes like enormous black marbles in his face. He was crying helplessly with fear, shouting urgently at his brother.

Ash wasn't crying. His face was blank. He was a boy, pale-faced and covered with acne, peering straight ahead, out of an endless nightmare.

Then I heard Rainbow's voice. 'Brake!' he was screaming at Ash. 'Brake brake brake!'

I didn't think. 'Brake!' I screamed back in the moment I heard the words.

I hit the brakes so hard I thought I'd broken my foot. I slammed down through the gears and heard the gearbox crashing into awful grating oblivion. The brakes squealed and screamed as I slowed. Smoke poured out of the exhaust. The speedometer was down to twenty miles an hour and I could smell the black smoke. I swerved hard to the left so that the car would hit the railings sideways on and not go through them. In a single decisive movement, I yanked at the handbrake and scrambled for the passenger door.

I was rolling before the car hit the railings. A savage pain jarred through my elbow. I heard the screech of metal and the rending crash of the Metro's gears, the howl of overheating brakes. I could smell burning tyres. But the Metro had not gone over the sea wall. It was on fire. I kept rolling, terrified that I was going to go straight underneath the railings and down to the freezing water, or burn to death in the conflagration. I did a forward roll, and was on my feet in seconds, stumbling and then finding my feet again and running away from the sea wall and the Metro. I was almost at the entrance to Wonderland when I heard the explosion. It rent the air. It sucked oxygen out of my lungs. I hit the floor, and was blasted by a wall of heat.

# Twenty-seven

There was a huge explosion and then it was over as suddenly as it had begun.

I held my breath. All I could hear was silence. I looked up. My own Metro was burning. Ash and Rainbow's car had disappeared.

'No!' I heard my voice tearing the cold night air. 'No!'

Then I was running.

I ran to the sea wall. I clambered up onto the top, the rough stone cutting my hands, grazing my knees. My jeans were ripped. My hands were wet with blood and salt water. I reached the top of the wall and stared down into the surging darkness. There was no sign of

Ash and Rainbow. There was nothing but the sea.

'Rainbow!' I wailed into the night. 'Ash!'

I could hear the foghorns out at the estuary, the sea pounding up the beach. I could hear the blood pounding in my ears. But nothing else. No calls. No screams. Nothing. I was alone.

'No!' I cried again into the wintry darkness. 'No! No! No!'

There was no car. It must have gone over the railings and straight into the sea, plunging beneath the waves in seconds. Nobody could have got out that quickly. They wouldn't have stood a chance. I took a deep breath and managed to stand. My head was swimming. My legs felt like rubber. I felt dizzy and confused, as if I'd just woken and found myself in a strange room, surrounded by a world I didn't know, or belong to.

I was lost. I was the only one who had survived. They might never have lived. Never have been born.

The railings were bent and buckled, but the concrete wall was unmarked. They had gone straight through the railings. There was no sign of life, no evidence of anything below the surface. The car had simply disappeared. Drowned in the deep waters.

Waves beat restlessly against the sea wall. I was soaked with spray. I leaned over and stared down into the sea, but there was no murmur of voices, no wreckage, no sign of my friends, Ash and Rainbow. They were gone.

'Gone!' I yelled in my pain.

My voice echoed out to sea, disturbing seagulls, bouncing back off the fog. A foghorn moaned at the estuary: gone, gone, gone.

'I don't understand,' I said aloud, my eyes filling with tears. Quite suddenly, I didn't feel so old. I felt like the fourteen year-old I was, and I wanted somebody to look after me.

I heard the police sirens turning down the promenade, and the fire engines, and saw the blue lights of an ambulance. I turned and walked away.

I kept walking, all the way home.